Date Due Slip

JAN 2 4 2005

MURDER IN A MUMMY CASE

We're back in the 1920s and K. K. Beck's delightful flapper, Iris Cooper, whom we met in *Death in a Deck Chair*, is again thrust into detection—this time while a house guest of the wacky Brockhurst family at their Californian mansion. Iris's beau, Clarence Brockhurst, collects Egyptian mummies, while Mother collects 'interesting' people. All the ingredients of a 1920s pastiche are here: a brash, fast-talking newshound, a madcap debutante, a mysterious Oriental butler, a slightly dubious spiritualist and more. When the spiritualist's maid is found dead in the mummy's casket the police are baffled—it's up to Iris and reporter Jack Clancy to solve the mystery.

MURDER IN A MUMMY CASE

K. K. Beck

ATLANTIC LARGE PRINT

Chivers Press, Bath, England.
John Curley & Associates Inc.,
South Yarmouth, Mass., USA.

Library of Congress Cataloging in Publication Data

Back, K. K.
    Murder in a mummy case / K. K. Back.
        p.   cm.—(Atlantic large print)
    1. Large type books.   I. Title.
[PS3552.E24M8   1989]   88–35027
813'.54—dc19   CIP

ISBN 1–55504–841–2 (pbk. : lg. print)

British Library Cataloguing in Publication Data

Beck, K. K. *1950–*
    Murder in a mummy case
    I. Title
    813'.54[F]

ISBN 0–7451–9460–5

This Large Print edition is published by Chivers Press, England, and
John Curley & Associates, Inc, U.S.A. 1989

Published in the British Commonwealth by arrangement with the author
and in the U.S.A. and Canada with Walker and Company

U.K. Hardback ISBN 0 7451 9460 5
U.S.A. Softback ISBN 1 55504 840 4

for the greatest mummy in the world
JEAN BECK
with love and thanks

All the characters and events portrayed in this story are fictitious.

MURDER IN A MUMMY CASE

CHAPTER ONE

I sat down at the little desk in the sitting room of the dormitory suite and unscrewed my fountain pen. It was with some trepidation that I wrote my aunt the following letter:

March 19, 1928
Stanford University
Palo Alto, California

Dear Aunt Hermione:

Would it be too disappointing if I didn't come home this Easter vacation? I can still return my train ticket. You see, Clarence Brockhurst (I've written you about him) has invited me to stay with his family over the holidays.

The Brockhursts live in Burlingame, just up the peninsula from here, about halfway to San Francisco. They are very respectable people. Mr. Brockhurst's family were pioneers in the railroad business, but he is now involved in various enterprises. Mrs. B. is an active club woman and rather artistic, I believe. There are a brother and sister too. But most important, Clarence is a very sincere young man, and we have formed the beginnings of an attachment. In fact, things have reached the point where I

1

feel it is important that I meet his family.

I suppose Father will make a fuss. I know he has been eager to take me on that trout-fishing trip up at the lodge. Can you put it to him with your usual tact?

I know I should have told you more about Clarence. I imagine I was waiting to see what my true feelings were. He's very handsome, with refined, chiseled features, an intelligent broad forehead and lovely blue eyes. He has thick dark hair and level, dark brows. He is studying Egyptology and he's already been on several archaeological expeditions. Last year he went up the Nile and excavated a tomb. In fact, when he asked me if I'd like to spend Easter vacation with his family, he said, "I'd like you to meet my mummy." I naturally thought he meant Mrs. Brockhurst, but actually he meant Ra-Hotep. Clarence's father would like him to go into business, but Clarence plans to spend his life racketing around the globe and digging up remains of ancient civilizations. Doesn't that sound absolutely wonderful?

I shall miss seeing you and the children, and Father too, of course, but it isn't much longer until summer vacation and then I'll be back in Portland for a long time.

Are Freddy's adenoids any better? I hope so. I agree with you that whatever happens it is wise to rely on Dr. Smith. If he says

2

they should come out, no doubt they should.

Love to all of you,
Iris

P.S. If it's all right for me to go to the Brockhursts, could you please send me the Nile-green moiré silk I left in the upstairs closet? I hope it doesn't smell of camphor. I have the impression the Brockhursts dress for dinner, and I only have the white tulle and the mauve chiffon.

I would miss seeing Aunt Hermione and the rest of my family, but I was awfully keen to meet the Brockhursts, mummy and all. I waited eagerly for my aunt to answer. Had I but known that my request would lead me into another adventure, my anticipation would have been even greater. As it was, I was delighted when Aunt Hermione wrote me by return mail.

March 25, 1928
Portland, Oregon

Dearest Iris,

While it is true, you hadn't written *too* much about the young man, I had already gathered, from what you *had* written, that you were developing more than a comradely feeling for a fellow student. It is all inevitable with all this co-education, I suppose, and perhaps it is a good thing too.

3

More *natural* somehow.

Still, you are quite young, Iris, and I hope you won't do anything *rash*, although I can't imagine you would. What I mean is, you still have *plenty* of time to settle down. In any case, I think it will be fine for you to visit the Brockhursts. (I trust you also received a formal invitation from Clarence's mother?)

I have already spoken with your father. He grumbled about the arrangements and would have liked to see you, but I was most forceful. I emphasized that you were a sensible girl who wouldn't go off and visit a young man's family on a mere *caprice*.

I also made a few discreet enquiries about the Brockhursts. (Olivia Nelson, you know, has connections in California.) She tells me that the Brockhursts have a *great deal* of money. I hope this does not mean that they are vulgar. In any case, I trust your judgment in such matters, as it is highly developed for a girl your age, no doubt because of all the responsibilities that fell upon you when your dear mother died.

Do have a lovely time, dear. If anyone deserves a gay and happy young womanhood, Iris, it is you.

I shall have the dress sent immediately. Please give me the Brockhursts' address, as I should like to write them a little note thanking them for having you and thereby letting them know you have my permission to be there. I've also enclosed an extra check for you to buy something nice for your hostess and to tip the servants with.

Do let me know how your visit goes.

As ever,
Aunt Hermione

We went up the peninsula to Burlingame by train. It was while Clarence and I were sitting on the green leather seats of the parlor car that I began to ask him about his family. 'Well,' said Clarence, perhaps, I thought, a little warily, 'Father is of course very preoccupied with business. He's disappointed I'm going to be an archaeologist and not follow in his footsteps. And Bunny, well, Bunny's a good girl, really, just awfully energetic. Goes to lots of parties, likes to have a good time. A thoroughly modern type of girl. I'm sure you'll like her, Iris. Once you get to know her, that is.'

This sounded rather ominous, but I simply smiled and said I was sure that was so.

Clarence frowned. 'I'm a little worried about Henry, to tell you the truth. He's only sixteen, but his intellectual capacities are highly developed. He's a real wiz. It's—well—sometimes I think there's something not entirely normal about Henry.'

'Oh, really?' I said expectantly.

'Perhaps his brain is overdeveloped,' said

5

Clarence with a puzzled air. 'He should get out of doors more, in the fresh air.'

'I see,' I said mildly.

'And then there's Mother.' Clarence sighed. 'Mother collects people. Interesting people.'

'How delightful,' I said.

'Well, sometimes they are *too* interesting,' he began. 'Frankly, Iris, I think sometimes they take advantage of her good nature. Right now,' he said, 'Mother's dabbling in spiritualism.'

'Oh, you mean Ouija boards and table turning?'

'I guess so.' He seemed a little vague. 'You'll meet Madame Sophie. She's been staying with the folks for some months now. She's a medium.'

'Really?' I felt my eyes grow round.

Clarence laughed a self-deprecating little laugh. 'Oh dear, Iris, I hope you won't think they're all too eccentric. After all, a nice wholesome normal girl like you . . .' He trailed off and gazed at me with a rather smitten look.

I was annoyed. I didn't really want to be thought of chiefly as wholesome and normal. It sounded simple. I was about to say something, but Clarence changed the subject. 'Oh, anyway, Iris, what does my family matter? It's you I want to be with. And there's so much for you to see. My mummy,

6

of course, and lots of shards. I thought if we had some spare time perhaps we could try and piece together some of them. It's painstaking work, but so rewarding. Like a giant jigsaw puzzle. I bet you'd be awfully good at it.' He took my hand and gave me another soulful gaze, and then the train pulled into Burlingame with a jolt.

On the platform, Bunny Brockhurst met us. She was about my age, and a little taller. Her smooth dark hair, so like Clarence's, was cut in a Dutch bob, shingled up the back with straight bangs across her forehead. Hatless, she wore a scarlet dress, showing a lot of leg in sheer stockings. Bunny had a lively face, a little kittenish, with an upturned nose and almond-shaped green eyes. Her wide mouth was crimsoned the same shade as her dress.

While I acknowledged Clarence's introduction and took in the above feminine details, Clarence was loading down an immaculately liveried elderly chauffeur with our luggage, tennis rackets, and Clarence's golf clubs.

'I was shopping in the city,' explained Bunny, 'so I arranged to come and fetch you on my way back. I hope you don't mind. The whole trunk of the car is loaded with parcels, but I'm sure Griswold can fit everything in.'

Griswold nodded silently to indicate that everything could be properly arranged, and Bunny led us to the car behind him.

7

'I'm so glad to meet you, Miss Cooper,' she began. 'It's so nice to have a fresh new face around. The old bunch can pall.'

'Is Boris still with us?' said Clarence.

'Of course. I'm sure he'll always be with us. At least until the Bolsheviks are kicked out of Russia.'

She turned to me. 'Boris is a White Russian, some kind of a duke Mother picked up in the south of France. Father says he was probably just a gigolo looking for something more permanent and less strenuous, but actually he was a majordomo at the Hotel Carlyle.

'The star boarder now is, of course, Madame Sophie. Did you warn Iris?'

'Really, Bunny, I shouldn't put it that way,' said Clarence, obviously annoyed with his sister's candor.

'Mother's *medium*,' said Bunny. 'And her entourage. They haven't let me in to see her stir up the spirits. Madame Sophie says I'm not pure enough.' Bunny laughed heartily. 'Apparently the spooks know all.'

Clarence looked uncomfortable at this line of talk, but Bunny rattled on as we arranged ourselves inside the very smart cabriolet and the chauffeur closed the door.

When the driver had taken the car slowly into traffic, Bunny seized the speaking tube and said, '*Please*, Griswold, we're not going to a funeral. Step on it, will you?'

8

'Griswold is really too old to drive properly,' Bunny said to me, as she replaced the instrument. 'He's lost his nerve. We had a much younger man, but Daddy got rid of him. Maurice was *very* good-looking,' she explained, 'and when Daddy found out he and I were secretly engaged . . .'

'Oh, really, Bunny,' said Clarence. 'Must we go on in this sordid vein?'

I had been rather enjoying Bunny's monologue, delivered in an amusing drawl, but I imagined poor Clarence wanted his family to make a more conventional impression on me.

'Oh, Clarence,' said Bunny, 'don't be so smug. You're in Dutch at home yourself.'

'What?' Clarence looked startled.

'Madame Sophie says your mummy is disturbing the emanations at the house, and now Mother's begun to worry about the spiritual aspects of having a rotting corpse lying around the place.'

'It's not *rotting*,' said Clarence firmly. 'It's perfectly mummified. And if this Madame Sophie thinks she can . . .' He sputtered a little, looked out the window, got himself under control again, and said loudly, 'Well, that's the *limit*.'

We were heading now past the little village of Burlingame and up a long winding road into the hills above. Presently we drove through a wide wrought-iron gate hung on two columns of stone. It was clear the Brockhursts lived very well indeed. Soon a landscape of tangled eucalyptus and wild California lilac gave way to more manicured grounds, and a sweep of emerald lawn led the eye to an imposing structure, a large stucco house in the style of a French chateau. A circular gravel drive led past a fountain encrusted with cherubs to the porte-cochère at the side.

Griswold, who had ignored Bunny's urgings to step on it, brought the car around the drive in such a decorous manner that I'm sure not a single bit of gravel was displaced.

Bunny bounded up the steps and Clarence and I followed, while Griswold behind us staggered under his amazing load of luggage, sporting equipment, and innumerable dress boxes.

A tall Chinese butler opened the door. He was perfectly turned out in striped trousers, a black swallowtail coat, a black waistcoat and a stiff-bosomed white shirt with a black four-in-hand. 'Madam is in the library,' he murmured, as he divested us of our wraps.

The library was a big square room with lots of chintz slipcovers, pleasant landscapes on the walls, and a few rows of glassed-in bookshelves with a collection of neglected-looking old books in ancient bindings. A circle of faces turned expectantly toward us, and Mrs. Brockhurst came forward. She was a rosy, plump lady with a look of firm, comfortable flesh about her. Her dark hair, touched lightly with gray, was dressed becomingly in waves around her face. She wore blue chiffon that floated around her ample but superbly corseted figure.

Mrs. Brockhurst embraced her children and took my hand between her two plump pink beringed ones.

'We're so glad to have you here, Miss Cooper,' she said. 'Clarence has told me so much about you and your passionate interest in Egyptology. How nice that young girls nowadays have intellectual interests.' She gave a worried look in the direction of Bunny, who was lingering in the hall arranging her bangs with her fingertips and smiling appreciatively at her reflection in a gilt-framed mirror.

'But come, you must meet everyone. The men are out playing golf, but you'll see them at cocktails.' She presented me to Madame Sophie, the medium, a cheerful-looking woman with a ruddy complexion, dressed in an odd arrangement of shawls and veils and primitive jewelry. Madame Sophie had fluffy white hair and a thick Cockney accent.

'And here is Clarence's Aunt Laura, my sister-in-law, Miss Brockhurst.' Clarence hadn't told me about this relative, but her self-effacing demeanor gave me the impression that perhaps Miss Brockhurst was

11

often forgotten. She was a grayish lady of indeterminate age with a disapproving little face and an antique tea gown in some sort of dark stuff cut in an old-fashioned style, pinched in at the waist and bunched out in the skirt. She also wore some old cameo earrings and thick lisle stockings that ended in peculiar flat shoes.

'And here is my youngest son, Henry.' Henry took after his mother, being rather plump for a boy his age. He had a solemn face behind round horn-rimmed spectacles with lenses so thick they made his eyes look enormous. His dark hair was parted precisely in the middle of his round head, a style that only emphasized the puffiness of his face.

'Now sit down beside me and have some tea,' Mrs. Brockhurst said cozily, 'before you go up to your room. Milk or lemon?'

Bunny flung herself into a chair and Clarence busied himself at the tea cart and prepared a plate of cakes and sandwiches for me as I accepted a teacup from his mother.

'I sense,' said Madame Sophie, leaning forward, 'that you may have psychic gifts. Have you Celtic blood?'

This was hardly evidence of Madame Sophie's gifts. I am very fair with red-gold hair and hazel eyes. 'My mother's family was Scottish,' I said warily. 'But I've never thought I was fey or anything like that.' Actually, I did think often that I was

12

intuitive, but I chalked it up to common sense and reasonably keen powers of observation.

'Are you, Miss Cooper,' persisted the old lady, 'a *believer?*'

I took the plate Clarence proferred and nervously said, 'Well, we're Episcopalians,' as I sipped my tea.

'God's house has many mansions,' said Madame Sophie sententiously.

'They're deciding whether or not you can come to a séance,' said Bunny abruptly, before biting into a cream cake.

'Oh, I'd love to,' I said eagerly. Really, the idea appealed to me enormously.

'Then you're not a skeptic?' said Mrs. Brockhurst pleasantly.

'Well, I don't know much about spiritualism,' I began. I didn't want to lie. I *was* skeptical. But if there were to be any rappings or table turnings, I wanted to see them for myself.

'*I* am a skeptic,' said Aunt Laura in a firm tone at odds with her meek appearance. 'I think it is a mistake to meddle with things of which Providence has apparently chosen we remain in ignorance.' She paused and then said with a trace of a whine: 'That's my opinion and there it is.'

'Oh, Laura,' said Mrs. Brockhurst, dismissing the little woman's heartfelt opinion with a wave and a trace of a laugh,

13

'Providence has evidently chosen we learn of these mysteries. Why else would He have given Madame Sophie her special gifts?'

'Why indeed?' said Madame Sophie smugly, as she adjusted about her shoulders a flopping fringed garment that looked like nothing less than a piano shawl.

Young Henry blinked behind his thick spectacles and said in a croaking adolescent voice: 'Dabbling in spiritualism represents an abandonment of the intellect. How can we resolve deep philosophical dilemmas in such a showy way?'

His mother frowned. 'Henry, why don't you go outside and play. Or perhaps there's some homework you can do.'

'I haven't any homework. It's spring vacation.'

'Well, then, go upstairs and clean your room. How about boxing up those old toys in the attic for the orphan asylum? You don't play with that electric train any more, do you?'

'I like to make crashes,' said Henry, selecting a large cake for himself and devouring it greedily.

Clarence's family was not as I had imagined it, I thought to myself. Clarence must have had similar thoughts, for he eyed them all before he rose abruptly and said, 'Come along, Iris, let's go upstairs and see my mummy. I know you're awfully keen on seeing it.'

'Whatever you do around here,' said Bunny, fitting a cigarette into an amber holder, 'you're going to have to come face to face with the undead—either floating around in ectoplasm or pickled in a mummy case.'

CHAPTER TWO

Clarence took me by the hand and led me up the curving staircase and then up one more flight to the attic. 'Here we are, Iris. A sort of pocket museum, you might call it.'

We entered this room—I made a point of leaving the door open only in case there were servants about who might gossip, as Clarence was an almost exasperatingly correct young man. There against the wall was an open sarcophagus, blessedly empty.

'I'm translating these hieroglyphs,' he said eagerly, indicating the ancient writing inside the mummy case. 'This was just one of the coffins, of course, within the stone sarcophagus. It was hermetically sealed. Ensured that the mummy within it was preserved for centuries—until I came along to dig it up. Incredible, isn't it? And here he is, in the flesh, so to speak, Ra-Hotep.' He directed me to a smaller case—one that had apparently been inside the first one we had examined.

I tried not to cringe as I inspected Ra-Hotep. The muslin had been partially unwrapped, to reveal the head and torso, bony arms demurely crossed against his chest. His eyes were gone, and his ears and nose had not been well preserved, but Ra-Hotep showed unmistakably human form. The bones of his skull and face strained against the ancient tanned skin, and the flesh had receded from a set of large teeth. I suppressed a shriek—it became a mere intake of breath.

In another adventure [see *Death in a Deck Chair*] I had seen two fresh corpses, corpses of people who had met violent ends. Somehow poor Ra-Hotep looked more pathetic. Perhaps, despite my knowledge that Clarence was a scientist in the purest sense, I felt that the body of this ancient and esteemed gentleman should have been more properly left beneath the desert sands.

Clarence seemed to notice my discomfiture. He put an arm around me and said, 'You're a plucky girl, Iris. Most people are more upset by this. Think of what we can learn from it. I know *you* understand.'

I laughed a little nervously and stepped back. 'Of course, Clarence,' I said.

'And over here,' said Clarence eagerly, 'is the hide of the old crocodile I shot.' Attached to another wall there hung a long and scaly crocodile skin. Above, on a peg, hung an old

16

revolver, similar to the one Father had carried in the Spanish-American War and which was kept in the safe in his office.

'Did I tell you about it?' he said.

He had, of course. The crocodile had been making its way toward some Egyptian women doing their laundry on the banks of the Nile, and Clarence had killed the beast with a single shot.

'And over here,' said Clarence, leading me to a low table which was really sort of a museum case with a glass lid, 'are some of the artifacts.' Inside were fabulous necklaces and bracelets in lapis lazuli, beautifully wrought and graceful despite their massiveness.

'Oh, they're lovely,' I said. 'Let me see them.'

He opened the glass top and selected a lovely greenish scarab ring. He took my hand and placed the ring on my finger. 'Iris,' he said impetuously, 'would you like to have this? As a token of my . . .'

I looked at him, startled, and then Bunny's voice came from the doorway. 'Mother wants me to show Iris her room,' she said.

'We'll see the shards later,' said Clarence.

I took the ring off my finger and thrust it into Clarence's hand. 'Of course. Yes.'

I was really flustered. What did Clarence mean by presenting me with a ring? Whatever he did mean, I felt uncomfortable and somehow sure that if he gave me one of

17

Ra-Hotep's treasures he might regret it someday. A fraternity pin might have been more appropriate.

Bunny came into the room, linked her arm through mine and took me down the softly carpeted hall and to a delicious little guest room, so peaceful and beautifully appointed, compared to my room at Roble Hall on campus, that I felt instantly entranced.

There was a bed with a satin eiderdown in periwinkle blue and a collection of delicate French Provincial furniture and a white bowl of lilacs. At the diamond-paned windows was an inviting window seat framed by chintz draperies in a rose pattern. My suitcases had been unpacked; my dresses hung in a cedar-lined closet, and my other things were neatly folded in a highboy with gilt pulls.

'Do you rise early?' asked Bunny. 'If you want breakfast in your room, just ring,'—she indicated a tapestried bell-pull near the bed—'but if you're the energetic type, there's breakfast between eight and ten in the dining room, with hot dishes and so forth. Do you have everything you need?' She inspected the bedside table and picked up a book which lay there. 'Oh, I see Mother has left you some Madame Blavatsky to read. *Isis Unveiled*.' She shuddered. 'I hope you brought something of your own.'

I had the newest mystery by S. S. Van Dine, thank goodness.

'Why don't you get settled and come down any time?' she said. 'Cocktails are at six-thirty.' I thanked her, and before she left the room she turned to me and said, 'Isn't Clarence's mummy simply awful?'

I was rather glad of a little time to myself. The Brockhurst family—what I had met of them so far in any case—seemed to me rather *intense*. I had to confess to myself that this observation included Clarence. Surely that scarab wasn't intended as an engagement ring. I had always fantasized about getting, when the time came, a simple stone in a simple setting—perhaps a sapphire, my birthstone. Suddenly I felt very young. I went to a little desk, where I found ivory-tinged letter paper. I sat down and began a letter to Aunt Hermione.

Dear Aunt Hermione,
Thank you so much for letting me come to the Brockhursts'. They are a very hospitable family—my room is lovely. So far, I haven't seen any evidence of the vulgarity you worried about, except maybe a rather baroque fountain with lots of fat cherubs on it. Somehow, though, in this climate it all looks riotously Mediterranean and not vulgar at all.
Clarence showed me his mummy. Clarence is a perfect gentleman in every respect, not at all like so many of the boys

19

on campus, and his interest in his field is really inspiring. His mother, Mrs. Brockhurst, couldn't have been nicer. There is also a sister and a brother. I haven't met Mr. B. yet.

There is a spiritualist on the premises, a medium named Madame Sophie. Frankly, I am hoping to be included in one of her séances. Don't you think it will be interesting?

I'll write more later—I've just arrived.

I put my letter in a drawer of the desk and lay back on the bed, thinking. Should I wear the white tulle and pearls or start out with the Nile-green moiré silk right off? I finally decided on the white tulle, and I went down a little nervously for cocktails.

The stairway to the main hall had a wide curve in it, and as I began to go down and turned the corner, I saw a maid in front of me. It wasn't just that she was using the main stairs that made her seem out of place. She positively sauntered down the stairs, like a belle on her way to a ball. And she had hair an unlikely shade of blonde. I was sure it was peroxided. I caught up with her, and on closer inspection I saw her nails were long and pointed and, except for the moons and tips, painted scarlet in the fashion of a demi-mondaine. This was all very odd in such a well-run household.

20

Waiting for us below was the butler Chan. He was carrying a tray of canapés. He frowned at the little maid and said to me: 'Cocktails are being served on the terrace off the library. Let me show you the way.'

As I prepared to follow him, he turned around and said to the peroxided blonde maid: 'Florence, please wait for me here. I need to speak to you.'

'No, I won't,' she said sharply. 'I don't take orders from no Chinaman.' She flounced off through a green baize door at the edge of the hall.

Chan stood immobile, his tray not moving an inch, his face a mask. While he betrayed no anger, the chill cast to his features, the set of his mouth and eyes, left no doubt he was intensely angry. And with good reason. I wondered if it were my duty to somehow let Mrs. Brockhurst know about the girl's insolence. It would have to be handled very carefully—through Clarence—or it would seem as if I was presuming to criticize the domestic arrangements. Still, I felt sorry for the butler.

'Is that one of the housemaids?' I asked him, wondering how anyone who worked with her hands could sustain such an elaborate manicure.

'No, Miss. That is Madame Sophie's *lady's* maid.' He lingered just long enough on the adjective to make me wonder if he weren't being sarcastic.

I was led out some French doors off the library to a flagstone area with a lot of wicker furniture and a festive red-and-white striped canopy overhead.

'There you are, Iris,' said Clarence, rushing toward me. 'Come, meet Father.'

Edgar Brockhurst was a tall, rather forbidding-looking man with a lantern jaw and intelligent eyes. He gave me a quick glance and a restrained smile. Mrs. Brockhurst rushed to our side. 'And you must also meet my husband's business acquaintance, Mr. Leonard.'

Mr. Leonard proved to be a bubbly, corpulent gentleman with a winning gleam in his eye, rather a contrast to the flintiness of Clarence's father.

'Oh, my, Clarence's friend is it?' he said waggishly, beaming at me in an avuncular way.

'Mr. Leonard,' said Mrs. Brockhurst, 'has shown an interest in spiritual matters. He'll be joining us at this evening's séance.'

'So you are a believer,' I said.

'I'm open-minded,' declared the little man. 'The powers in the mind are a great untapped resource.' He positively bubbled.

'I'm sure that's true,' I said vaguely.

Mr. Leonard smiled and waved his cocktail glass.

'"Every day in every way I am better and

better,"' he quoted, though what Mr. Coué's sentiment had to do with spiritualism I wasn't sure.

'And you haven't met Boris,' said Clarence, drawing me away.

Boris, the grand duke, was an attractive man in his late forties with silvery hair, a tanned face, and a magnificent waxed moustache. He looked lovely in evening clothes and greeted me with a flourish, rolling his *r*'s in an intriguing way. There was something a little sad about his eyes.

I nodded to Madame Sophie, Clarence's Aunt Laura, and Henry, who was making free with the canapés. Bunny came up to us wielding a silver cocktail shaker. 'I've sent Chan away,' she said. 'I adore mixing cocktails myself. Well, are you coming to the séance tonight?'

'I'd love to,' I said breathlessly. 'Do you think I'll be allowed?'

She gave me a significant look. 'You bet,' she said with a wink. 'Daddy just arranged with Mummy for everyone to come tonight. Mr. Leonard egged him on. So all of us will be allowed.'

I turned to Clarence. 'Oh, won't it be thrilling?' I said.

'I guess so.' He looked dubious. 'But I don't know, Iris, the whole thing gives me the creeps. Oh, here's Mr. Jones. Madame Sophie's private secretary.'

23

A sleek, dark man in his thirties came forward and was introduced. He had obviously overheard, for he said smoothly: 'You mustn't be alarmed, Clarence. Madame Sophie has demonstrated her powers many times, before all kinds of skeptics. It is a special strain on her, but it is sometimes necessary.'

There was something very attractive yet simultaneously repellent about Mr. Jones. I was dying to know just what he did for Madame Sophie. Did a medium need a secretary? He must have been very intuitive, for he seemed to catch my puzzled look and said, 'Madame Sophie, like many sensitives, is delicate. She needs someone to help her—to handle her many requests for sittings and so forth, and her business interests as well. I am privileged to serve her in that way, as well as to assist at the séances themselves.'

'I see. It must be interesting work,' I said.

Clarence nodded rather perfunctorily at Mr. Jones and took me by the elbow. 'Let me show you the grounds,' he said.

I let him lead me away, but not before taking a cocktail proffered by the solemn Chan.

'Well,' said Clarence, when we had passed from the flagstones to a velvety lawn, 'what do you think of my family? Wait. Don't say anything yet. I know they seem a little eccentric. All except Father, of course. He's

MK

not eccentric at all. If he were more eccentric maybe the rest of us wouldn't be.'

'Oh, Clarence,' I said, goggling at him above the rim of my glass as I took a sip, *'you* aren't eccentric.' I gazed down at my glass. 'Is there gin in this?'

'Not to worry,' said Clarence reassuringly. 'Nothing bathtub about it. Chan manages to get the very best stuff. From Canada or something. We don't ask.'

'Well, as long as I won't go blind,' I said recklessly, and took another sip. 'You don't think he could get a few bottles of decent sherry for Aunt Hermione? She'd be thrilled.'

'I'm sure he could,' said Clarence. 'He's a remarkable man.'

He took me by the hand and led me even farther from the others. I hoped we weren't conspicuous. 'Here's the pool, around here,' he said. 'I hope I told you to bring a bathing suit.'

He hadn't, but I had anticipated they might have a pool and had brought one—rather itchy and heavy—that Aunt Hermione had knitted for me.

'And here,' he gestured, 'are the statues Mother brought from Greece.' We spent quite some time admiring a row of classical marble statues.

'Copies, I think, but I haven't the heart to tell her,' said Clarence. We laughed, and in that laugh there was a rather pleasant moment

25

of intimacy.

'Iris,' he said huskily, leaning toward me.

'Yes?' I said, looking up at him expectantly, but the elusive moment was broken by a stifled moan from a wicker sofa by the pool. We looked toward it and caught a glimpse, in the dusk, of a reclining Bunny entwined in the arms of someone in black dinner clothes.

I turned away instinctively, and Clarence said perhaps we'd better go back to the terrace. Who, I wondered, was that, petting on the wicker sofa with Bunny? Clarence and I both pretended we hadn't seen a thing.

At dinner my curiosity was satisfied. It was clear that Madame Sophie's secretary, the sleek, dark Mr. Jones, was receiving a lot of coy little glances from Bunny. On closer inspection I discovered a smudge of Bunny's crimson lip rouge on his collar.

CHAPTER THREE

Bunny had been right. Everyone was invited to this evening's séance. I had learned over dinner that Mrs. Brockhurst had extracted a promise that all skeptical remarks be stifled in exchange for the opportunity to attend. Mr. Brockhurst seemed already to be suppressing his disapproval, but Mr. Leonard waved his plump fingers in the air and said: 'Can't imagine how interesting this should be. It's a fascinating age we live in, eh, Brockhurst? Can't stop progress. Who knows, there might be a scientific basis to it all. Think of the commercial possibilities!'

Madame Sophie—I felt strange not knowing the rest of her name—intimated that the job of performing before a large group of skeptics would be trying but that she was up to the task.

After coffee we went to a small room fitted out with heavy blue velvet draperies at the windows. There was a thick Oriental carpet underfoot and, in the center of the room, a heavy mahogany table surrounded by chairs. Otherwise the room seemed bare of furniture, except for a strange, tall cabinet where Madame Sophie apparently sat during her séances.

Mr. Jones, who went among us murmuring facts about his employer's mediumship, explained it. 'She is very sensitive to the light—it disturbs her emanations—so she prefers to work from within this cabinet.' We examined it. It looked like a simple box with back, sides and roof, and appeared to be made of metal. There were gaudy symbols painted on the sides and a step led up to a velvet-lined chamber with a wooden chair and a collection of stout ropes. Mr. Jones explained that Madame Sophie would deign to be tied during the séance. 'This way she cannot be held accountable for fraudulent rappings or manifestations.'

'Manifestations?' I said.

Mr. Jones smiled. 'Many mediums in the past have produced astounding effects. Spirits are manifested, as are parts of their bodies and musical instruments or flowers— symbolic messages, perhaps, from the other side. Formed, of course, in ectoplasm.'

Mrs. Brockhurst looked quite eager. 'Once there was a hand,' she said gleefully, 'floating in the air and beckoning. I took it as a sign that I was being encouraged to develop my interest in the spirit world.'

Mr. Brockhurst snorted, and his wife gave him a pout. 'Come on, Edgar, we agreed. Afterwards you may say what you like, but not until then.'

'Most interesting, most interesting,' said the rotund Mr. Leonard. He passed a pudgy hand over an expanse of stomach and fiddled with a Phi Beta Kappa key that hung on his watch chain. He observed Mr. Jones tying Madame Sophie to a chair. She looked quite cheerful about it, shifting bits of her shawl around and settling cozily in her chair, despite the indignity of being bound up.

'I want to examine those ropes,' said young Henry Brockhurst defiantly. He went over and poked and prodded at the knots and declared them all tight and sound.

'Tell us about this ectoplasm,' said Mr. Leonard.

'A substance,' declared Madame Sophie, 'that comes from my nose and mouth—from any opening in the body, actually.' She paused while this indelicate fact sunk in. 'Ectoplasm forms the shapes of the departed. It is tiring work for me to produce it, but the rewards are so great—the comfort to us all to know that life is indeed eternal and that the dead never really die.'

'And now,' began Mr. Jones, pulling his cuffs back a little in a gesture I'd seen magicians make before they pulled rabbits out of hats, 'let us all sit in a circle. Remember, we must all hold hands to keep the spiritual force working its way through the circle.'

'Also,' added Mr. Brockhurst, 'we can make sure no one gets up and carries on like a ghost.'

'There is that too,' said Mr. Jones easily. 'First of all, before we dim the lights, let me light a little incense. It is a great help to Madame Sophie in creating the proper atmosphere.' He placed a wafer in a small brass object on the table and lit it. Soon, smoky fumes with a sandalwood scent began to rise.

We all sat down at the table—I was between Clarence and Aunt Laura, who had been pursing her lips with disapproval through all the preparation.

Mr. Jones went over to the lights, turning them off and leaving on just a small, dimly lit lamp in the corner with a green glass shade, making it possible to see things only as big dark shapes in the room.

A blue curtain with strange symbols embroidered on it in silver beads was pulled across the front of the little cabinet where Madame Sophie sat, a few feet from our table.

After a second or two, Bunny began to giggle. At least I assume it was Bunny. This was followed by a loud *shhhh* from someone. We sat silent for a moment, and perhaps it was from holding them up, but my hands started to tingle as if they were falling asleep. The incense began to make my eyes water. I was becoming uncomfortable, and I wondered how long it would be before the spirits came, if indeed they ever did.

A few moments later, from the medium's cabinet, we heard a crackle, almost like lightning, accompanied by a horrible little scream. The dim lamp across the room promptly went out and we were plunged into darkness. The incense seemed suddenly stronger.

I instinctively rose to see if Madame Sophie was all right, but Clarence pulled me back down, and Aunt Laura, on the other side of me, held on like death, so I sat again.

'Curious,' said Mr. Jones.

Suddenly, from the cabinet came a series of raps which went on and on, developing in intensity and frequency until they came in a staccato rhythm. Then they subsided.

'Raps,' whispered Mrs. Brockhurst, 'are easy. They are the easiest form of phenomena to get.'

But though we waited, there were no other phenomena for us to hear or observe. I was terribly disappointed. I had hoped at least for the beckoning hand, or perhaps tambourines and horns played by phantom hands.

Instead, after a pause, Mr. Jones spoke up. 'Tell us,' he said, 'if there are any spirit messages for us here.'

Madame Sophie, in her own Cockney voice but in a more leaden tone, began:

'The spirits are restless tonight. The messages are very difficult to read, very unclear. There is a curse on this house.'

Madame Sophie paused again and then warmed to her theme. 'An entity lies dead here, and wishes proper burial and respect for his earthly husk. Until that is done the manifestations will be, er, irregular.'

Madame Sophie sounded a little worried about the whole thing. At least I had imagined we were listening to Madame Sophie. I was corrected a moment later when Mr. Jones called out: 'Who are you?'

The reply was: 'I am little Alice, Madame Sophie's spirit guide. I have messages for

31

several of you, but the curse makes it harder—oh, my, it's as if a heavy veil has come down over you all. And we do so want to communicate. It is beautiful here on the other side.'

'Little Alice is the most adorable child,' said Mrs. Brockhurst. 'She's been manifested before. So sad. She died on the Lusitania.'

'I fear I am tiring poor Madame Sophie,' lisped the voice of Alice in her Cockney accent. 'But I have a message for Iris.' I sat bolt up. 'From a lady. She has lots of fair hair, parted in the center and tied up. She has large solemn eyes and a sweet smile.'

'That's Mother,' I heard myself say.

'Iris, dear, she wants you to know how happy she is, how glad she is dear Hermione has taken you under her wing. It's so beautiful here, Iris, you mustn't worry about her.' I didn't know what to think. Could it have been a real message? I felt confused and rather unhappy and melancholy, thinking how tantalizing these little bits and pieces of communication were.

'Oh, dear,' little Alice rattled on. 'I've tried to show myself to you and to answer your questions, but I simply cannot. Clarence, you must give the soul of poor Ra-Hotep some peace.'

'Maybe he'd be happier in a museum,' suggested Mrs. Brockhurst gently.

Next to me Aunt Laura sniffed. 'Or

perhaps he'd like a good Christian burial,' she said.

'Really, Aunt Laura,' snapped Clarence, 'the man died over a thousand years before Christ, so how could he have even known what a Christian burial was, let alone want one?'

The spirits cut short this domestic squabbling. 'Oh *Boris*,' said little Alice now, 'Boris, you have had much suffering. I see blood, an ocean of blood, rolling across a continent, across the steppes and sands of Russia.'

The Grand Duke Boris gave a loud sniff, as if he were about to burst into tears. 'Poor Russia,' he said, his voice full of feeling, 'oh, my poor Russia.'

'Czar Nicholas is here,' said little Alice casually. 'And the Czarina too. They are very happy here. It is lovely here, lovelier than anything you can imagine.'

'Why can't we see you tonight, Alice?' asked Mr. Jones rather firmly, as if trying to get a little child to do as it's told.

'I don't know,' said Madame Sophie in what sounded more like her own voice, and genuinely puzzled. 'The emanations are not themselves tonight. I can't get through. Don't understand . . .' She trailed off.

'I think that's enough,' said Mr. Jones crisply. 'I believe she has come out of her trance. Henry, if you would turn on the

33

lights?'

Aunt Laura let go of my hand, but Clarence held onto mine while we heard Henry crashing about in the dark. After a while we heard him say: 'It won't go on. The light switch isn't working properly. I guess I better go out and get a light of some kind.'

'Strange,' said Mr. Brockhurst. 'And that small lamp was extinguished too, just as Madame Sophie went into her trance.'

'There are powerful forces at work here,' said Mr. Jones. I heard another giggle from Bunny and wondered if Mr. Jones were using the darkness as an opportunity to exert his own powerful forces on Bunny, just as Clarence had taken the opportunity of holding my hand.

'Well, it's annoying,' snapped Mr. Brockhurst. 'There's no reason for this—no electrical storm or anything. Why, we have the most modern and up-to-date wiring.'

'Ah, but the forces of the spirit world are even stronger,' said Mrs. Brockhurst.

'Someone should check on Madame Sophie,' I said. It seemed discourteous to leave her tied up in the dark like that.

'I'm all right, ducks,' she piped up cheerfully.

The door to the room opened with a creak, and there stood Chan, holding a candelabra full of dripping white tapers. The light from the flames cast shadows all around the room and illuminated the butler from below, giving a sinister cast to his impassive features.

Behind him, Henry brandished a heavy metal flashlight, which he flickered all around the room in an unsettling manner, obviously enjoying himself thoroughly.

'We seem to have blown a fuse,' said Chan solemnly. 'I've arranged for the library to be lit. If you would all be so kind as to follow me to the sitting room, I will see about the lights.'

'I'll see about Madame,' said Mr. Jones, and prepared to draw back the blue beaded curtain. But Mr. Leonard, despite his girth, positively scampered over and said waggishly, 'Oh, let me do that, will you? I'd like to make sure the bonds are still tight. You won't mind?'

'Not at all,' said Mr. Jones, bowing slightly with a little gesture of the hand toward the cabinet, looking again like a stage magician.

'Most interesting, most interesting,' said Mr. Leonard. He undid the ropes by the light of Chan's candelabra while the rest of us looked on.

'There, you see,' said Mrs. Brockhurst. 'She's been tied up the whole time.'

I found nothing remarkable about this, as nothing had occurred which required that Madame Sophie be untied. The rappings could have come from her chair, I supposed, and the blown fuse must simply be coincidence.

I remained disturbed at the message from Mother. Could Madame Sophie have picked up some fragment of information from beyond the grave? The description was very like Mother. Instinctively I reached to touch the locket I usually wore around my neck, with Mother's picture in it. Then I remembered I'd taken it off to wear my pearls with the white tulle dress. It lay on the dresser in my room. And with a start, I realized that the letter I had begun to Aunt Hermione was in the small desk there. It would have been easy for anyone making a cursory search of the room to come up with enough information from the letter and the locket to have put together the simple spirit message for me. I shuddered at the thought of anyone going through my things.

Madame Sophie was now holding out her wrists for us to examine the reddish marks the ropes had left there, and displaying her thick ankles for similar inspection. The expression on her face, a rather foolish smile of childish pleasure at the attention she was receiving, was unnerving. I looked away. Foolish people often did the most harm, I reflected, thinking how painful one of her spirit messages could be to someone crazed by grief.

Presently, Chan led us down the hall and back to the library, now all tricked out with a collection of alcohol lamps which gave a rather cozy glow to the place. Outside it was still a little dusky—the darkness in the séance room had been in large part because of the heavy draperies at the window.

'Well, Clarence,' said Mrs. Brockhurst, sitting down heavily, 'I hope you took to heart what we learned about the mummy upstairs.'

'Oh really, Mother,' said Clarence irritably, 'it's all such a lot of *claptrap*.'

'Please, Clarence,' said his mother firmly. To Madame Sophie, who sat regally in a winged chair with Mr. Jones at her side, she said: 'I'm sure Clarence doesn't mean that.'

'Well, Daddy, what do you think?' said Bunny with a gleam of amusement in her eye. 'Perhaps you can ask for business advice next time. Maybe the spirits know which stocks are going to rise and what land to buy.'

'I've done just fine in business using plain common sense,' said Mr. Brockhurst. 'The character of the people involved is usually the best indicator of the soundness of an investment.'

'Well, if you insist I make other arrangements for Ra-Hotep,' began Clarence, 'I suppose . . .'

'He is unsettling,' said Mrs. Brockhurst. 'And you know the servants won't dust in there anymore.'

'I'll think about it,' said Clarence. 'In fact,

I had planned to take everything back down to Stanford, but not before I've studied it myself. If my professors get their hands on my material, I'll be pushed aside. I plan to translate the remainder of the hieroglyphs and work on the shards too. Iris says she'll help me with that,' he added brightly.

I smiled and tried to look noncommittal. Actually I had promised no such thing, and the work sounded unbearably tedious. Still, I tended to be indulgent. After all, Clarence was so keen on his work he just naturally assumed I was too.

'You are taking this all too lightly,' said Madame Sophie querulously. *There is a curse on that mummy*. How can you deny it?'

'Well, that's true,' said Clarence. 'There was a curse on the seal to the tomb. But that's standard on these tombs.'

'What about King Tut?' said Bunny. 'There was a curse on him. People died, didn't they?'

'Oh, what nonsense,' said Clarence.

'It's simply unchristian,' said Aunt Laura primly.

'Oh, *that*'s not the point,' said Mrs. Brockhurst, waving her hand impatiently at her sister-in-law. 'It's the curse we're concerned with, not the old thing's funeral arrangements.'

Madame Sophie held up a long bony finger and said dramatically: 'If the mummy is not

38

removed from this house, I may have to leave.'

I thought I caught a glimer of grim satisfaction on Mr. Brockhurst's lantern-jawed features. He certainly said nothing to dissuade Madame Sophie from leaving.

'Oh, don't worry about a thing,' said Mrs. Brockhurst. 'I'm sure we can make some suitable arrangements.' She gave Clarence a maternal glare.

'As for now,' continued Madame Sophie, waving a chiffon scarf in the air with a weary air, 'I must rest. My powers have been sorely taxed tonight.

'Raymond, perhaps if you could help me . . .'

Mr. Jones escorted the white-haired lady from the room, just as the lights flickered back on. The departure of the medium and her assistant and the illumination of the room in electric light changed the tense mood of the gathering immediately.

'Really, Bunny,' said Mr. Brockhurst, going over to a sideboard and browsing among a collection of decanters there, 'I wish you hadn't brought up business. The last thing I want is that woman meddling in. Mr. Leonard and I are about to launch an important enterprise, and we certainly don't need any advice from anyone. Do we Leonard?'

'We certainly don't,' said Mr. Leonard

affably. 'No, we don't need a crystal ball to see how profitable our association will be.' He rubbed his hands together gleefully. 'Real estate in California, a real gold mine,' he added.

Mr. Brockhurst frowned a little. 'Well, no need to bore the ladies with business details, is there? I feel like a small brandy. Would anyone care to join me?'

'I think she's a fake,' announced young Henry suddenly. 'I've been thinking about it, and, Mother, you're being duped. It would have been easier to prove it if she'd manifested those things you've claimed to see.'

'Don't be impertinent, Henry dear,' said Mrs. Brockhurst, arranging some cushions behind her.

'We should take photographs of the things she makes appear, and perform other scientific tests. I've already planned some,' he added.

'Henry, really,' said Mrs. Brockhurst. 'You're such a little materialist. Shouldn't you be off to bed now?'

Henry sulked out of the room after mumbling a few surly good-nights.

At a little table off to the side, Duke Boris and Aunt Laura were playing cribbage on a funny old-fashioned ivory cribbage board. 'She may be a fake,' said the grand duke, touching his moustache thoughtfully as he contemplated the game, 'but there are such things as spirits, and it is wise to give her the benefit of the doubt. I have seen too much in my life to scoff.'

I wondered drily if the grand duke weren't obliged to agree with Mrs. Brockhurst about most things if he were to remain under her roof. From what I had gathered, he was charming but impoverished, and stayed with the Brockhursts on a more or less permanent basis.

Chan came back a little later, took away the coffee and brandy things, and tidied up the ashtrays. 'We won't be needing you any more tonight,' Mr. Brockhurst said to him, and he bowed and left.

I stifled a yawn. I wanted to go to bed too. I had thought I might be wanted for bridge after dinner, but the séance was apparently the only item on the agenda. I felt justified in excusing myself to write a letter, and went upstairs.

I was halfway up when I noticed Clarence bounding up after me. To tell the truth, I was slightly disappointed. I wanted to get into my pajamas and finish Aunt Hermione's letter in bed, and then read myself to sleep. There was something awfully energetic about the Brockhurst family, and I wanted to be by myself for a while.

'Oh, Iris,' he said, taking my hand. 'I hope you're all right. Frankly, I'm rather sorry

Mother dragged you to that séance. It's all a little embarrassing, don't you think?'

'Well, I'm still a skeptic,' I said. 'But I wouldn't have missed it for the world. I was awfully curious.'

'That message about your mother,' he began awkwardly.

It was, I decided, rather cruel if it were fake, which I was sure it was. Apparently, Clarence felt the same way.

'I felt badly about that,' he said. 'Oh, I hope you don't think my family is impossible.'

'Not at all,' I said, not altogether truthfully. 'They've been very kind. I admit, though, the séance did give me the creeps.' I didn't add that it did so because I suspected someone had searched my room.

'Really? Poor Iris.' Clarence put his arms around me and then, from the wall behind me, I heard a horrible creaking noise.

I jumped.

Clarence laughed. 'Oh, don't mind that. It's just the dumbwaiter. It runs along behind that wall. Say, Iris, I've just had a swell idea. Why don't we go work on the shards now? Want to?'

I touched my forehead delicately with the back of my wrist. 'Oh, Clarence, that sounds wonderful, but I'm so tired, and I have a slight headache. I think I'd better go to bed.'

'Oh, all right.' Clarence looked

disappointed. He kissed my brow, and I went up to my room.

CHAPTER FOUR

About two hours later I had finished my letter to Aunt Hermione, full of details about the séance, and I had finished the detective novel I was reading. I felt a little guilty all the while for having had such a pleasant time tucked in with a book while Clarence was thinking I had a headache.

I had turned out the light and snuggled down under the eiderdown when I heard a rapping at the door and Clarence's loud whisper.

'Iris? Are you awake?'

I got up, put on my striped lavender kimono and went to the door.

Outside, Clarence stood there, also in pajamas and robe. 'Oh, Iris,' he began impetuously, 'I just couldn't sleep. I had to see you.'

I certainly had no intention of letting him in, but I was thrilled that Clarence had been moved enough to creep through the halls in his pajamas in search of me.

I smiled up at him in the half-light. 'Clarence, we really should go to bed. In our *own* beds, I mean,' I added hastily. 'It must

43

be the middle of the night.'

'Is your headache gone?' he asked, returning my smile.

'Yes, but Clarence . . .'

'Listen, Iris, I want to talk to you. You know that ring I tried to give you? The scarab?'

'Yes.'

'Well, I wouldn't want you to think it meant . . .'

'Meant what?'

'Well, dash it all, Iris, I guess it's no secret I'm crazy about you.'

I nodded. 'I had hoped so anyway.'

'You had? Well, listen, Iris, we're both awfully young . . .'

'Yes,' I said solemnly, 'we are.'

'And I don't want to ask you to marry me right now,'—he blurted this out with some difficulty—'but I want you to maybe *think* about it just a little. So I wouldn't want you to think the scarab is an engagement ring or anything, it's just that . . .'

'Oh, heavens, no,' I said, although I had thought just that.

'But I want you to keep it in mind. And I want you to wear something from me. Can I give you that scarab now, Iris?'

'Well, I suppose so,' I said rather dubiously, 'as long as it's clear there's nothing official.'

'You see, Iris,' said Clarence, 'I know

you're not sure yet, even if I am—I think, anyway. But maybe you could get used to the idea if . . .'

The nuances of the ring and our relationship as outlined by Clarence were becoming more and more confusing to me. To cut the conversation short, I finally said: 'Fine, Clarence. I'll wear the ring. But of course it isn't a gift. It's much too valuable, and I couldn't accept it. But if it will make you happy, I will wear it for a while.'

'Swell,' said Clarence. 'Let's go get it now, shall we?'

I was so unused to such impetuousness from Clarence that I agreed, and we set out, hand in hand, up the wooden stairs to the attic room where Clarence's Egyptian artifacts were kept. We giggled a little—it was rather fun to be sneaking around the house all by ourselves in our pajamas.

Once we entered the little room, Clarence switched on the light and I began to head for the glass case where the jewelry was kept. He lifted the lid, took out the ring, and placed it on my finger. He leaned over me, as if to kiss me, then suddenly he straightened up and cried out. 'Someone's been in here. I'm very particular about that. Nothing here must be touched.'

I looked around. Nothing looked different to me. 'What is it?' I said.

'Look! That mummy case is closed. I left it

45

open so as to decipher the hieroglyphs inside.' He strode over angrily to the mummy case, which stood on end against the wall, and lifted away the lid. I let out a scream and Clarence gasped and leaped back, but not before the corpse fell into his arms.

Rigid, rather like an ironing board emerging from a kitchen wall, a body had fallen out of the case. It was the pale white body of a woman, dressed in peach-colored satin step-ins and camisole trimmed with lace. The face was drained and lifeless. It was from the peroxide blonde hair and the red fingernails on small well-formed hands that I recognized the little lady's maid I'd observed earlier that evening, the one who Chan had explained was Madame Sophie's maid.

There was no question she was dead. Her pale blue eyes were open in a wide stare and her jaw was held in a rigid spasm. Clarence gently pushed the body back into the mummy case. 'What should we do now?' he said, almost as pale as the corpse.

'We must sound the alarm,' I said fully aware that it would be embarrassing to have everyone know Clarence and I were creeping around together in the night, but knowing, nevertheless, my duty. 'I'll stay here,' I said. 'Get the others.'

It was well after midnight and everyone was asleep. Clarence busied himself with rapping on doors and calling out that he'd found a body. It wasn't really necessary to awaken everyone. All that was really required was that we call the police. But I had convinced Clarence to round everyone up because I thought it might be important to see everyone's reaction to the discovery of the body.

I didn't know if the young woman had met with foul play—there wasn't a mark on the body that I could see—but I found it very odd that she was inside the mummy case. If in the normal course of things she had had some sort of an attack and collapsed and died—well, that was possible, if not probable. But that a girl should step into a mummy case in her underthings and then close the lid on herself before dying, well *that* seemed very peculiar indeed.

I tried not to touch anything. In fact, I just stood there and looked at the poor girl staring out at me from the mummy case. I suppose I should have been frightened, but to be quite honest, I was so interested in how and why the body came to be there, in Clarence's mummy case, that I forgot to be frightened.

A second later I was startled to see Ra-Hotep's brown-skinned skull grinning at me. I had forgotten all about him, and the sight of two corpses facing me suddenly struck me as rather horrible. I stepped backward from the room and into Clarence's arms.

47

'Oh, it's terrible,' I began, discovering myself shaking.

He put his arms around me and patted me on the back. 'I know, Iris, it is dreadful. I shouldn't have left you here alone. I can't imagine what came over me. Can you forgive me?'

'Let *me* see,' said Bunny, behind him. I disentangled myself from Clarence's arms and let Bunny by. She was wearing black silk pajamas. I couldn't help but notice, rather decadent-looking, and showing off her fashionably flat, boyish figure to perfection. One look at the little maid in her sarcophagus and Bunny let out a blood-curdling scream.

Clarence began to pat *her* on the back, and then we were joined by Mr. and Mrs. Brockhurst in their bathrobes.

'Clarence,' said his father sharply, 'what is this girl doing in your room up here?' he said, pointing to the body.

'That's what *I'd* like to know,' said Clarence indignantly. 'No one is supposed to tamper with my artifacts.'

Mrs. Brockhurst nibbled nervously on the tips of her fingers and said: 'We must do something.'

'Yes,' said Mr. Brockhurst. 'We must call the police. We don't know what happened to this young woman, and it is a job for the police. 'Let's all clear out of here now and I'll telephone.' He led us all back toward the

48

stairs, but as we prepared to descend, Madame Sophie, wearing a voluminous Victorian-looking nightdress, her white fluffy hair down and flowing over her shoulders, clomped up toward us.

'What is this all about?' she demanded.

Mrs. Brockhurst tried to prevent her from seeing. 'It's your maid. She's dead. There's nothing we can do for her now,' she said simply.

Madame Sophie shook off Mrs. Brockhurst's hand and peered into the room and into the gaping coffin.

'I knew it,' she said, pointing a long bony finger, her voice rising a little, an edge of hysteria creeping into it. 'It's the curse. The mummy's curse. It's killed Florence.'

'Let's go downstairs,' said Mr. Brockhurst firmly. 'I will call the police. Someone get Chan while I'm calling. I want him to lock up the wine cellar and the liquor cabinet. No use bringing the Volstead Act down on us if the police come to investigate.'

'Good thinking, Pop,' said Bunny. 'I'll take care of that.'

Out in the hall, Mr. Leonard and Raymond Jones were standing around, looking confused. Henry was there too.

'I see you roused everyone,' said Mr. Brockhurst to Clarence, rather irritably.

'That was my suggestion,' I said evenly. 'I thought the situation was rather serious.

49

Something very strange has happened to that girl.'

He looked at me perhaps for the first time, and seemed to understand what I was trying to convey—that perhaps one of us was responsible somehow and that everyone had to be accounted for.

'What's going on?' demanded Mr. Leonard.

Clarence explained that he had discovered a corpse in his mummy case. 'Madame Sophie's maid,' he said. 'Shocking, isn't it?'

'My, my,' said Mr. Leonard. 'It certainly is.' His usually bubbly face looked suitably grave.

'How *horrible*,' said Raymond Jones. 'What on earth can have happened?' I noticed that his brilliantined hair was perfectly in place. Down the hall, Aunt Laura popped her head out of her bedroom door. Her hair was done up in old-fashioned kidskin hair curlers. 'What's going on?' she demanded.

'I didn't want to disturb you, Aunt Laura,' said Clarence. Once again he'd forgotten about Aunt Laura. I don't know how she felt, but *I* would have been highly indignant if someone had discovered a dead body and failed to let me know at once.

The Grand Duke Boris stumbled sleepily out of his room, and Aunt Laura firmly popped back into hers like a cuckoo into its clock, and shut her door. Boris wore an absolutely fabulous maroon silk dressing gown with a crest on the pocket. It was so sumptuous that I imagined either Mr. Brockhurst was right, Boris had been a gigolo and had been presented this incredible garment by a grateful client, or the duke had managed to get his dressing gown out of Imperial Russia in 1917. Boris took a few steps, rustling taffeta all around him. 'Oh, Boris, it's too dreadful. Madame Sophie's little maid. She's dead,' exclaimed Mrs. Brockhurst. Around Boris's neck I observed a strange black object on an elastic band. After puzzling over it for some few seconds I decided it was a fixe-moustache, designed to keep his moustache pointing in the right direction through the night.

'I tell you, it's the mummy's curse,' shrieked Madame Sophie. Mr. Brockhurst, who had gone away to telephone, came back at this juncture, and I thought I saw him grind his teeth a little and give Madame Sophie an annoyed glance. 'Well,' he said, 'there's no need to stand around in the hall. The police are sending a man up here. I'll go downstairs and wait.'

'I guess Clarence and I should wait too,' I said. 'We found the body.' I wasn't going to miss any of this for the world.

'I suppose so,' said Mr. Brockhurst. 'Maybe we can get Chan to rustle up some cocoa or something.'

51

Mr. Leonard and Mr. Jones went back to bed, as did the Grand Duke Boris. Mrs. Brockhurst led Madame Sophie away, presumably to sit with her a while. The medium seemed very upset—not so much, it seemed, that her maid had died, but rather because she feared the mummy's curse.

'I want to wait up too,' said Henry, polishing his spectacles on the lapels of his bathrobe. 'It will be enlightening to see actual police methods, and whether or not they differ from detective stories.

'It seems to me,' he continued, 'that psychology should be used to expose criminal activity.' He put on the glasses and looked around. 'Do you think she was murdered?' he demanded. 'It must be some sex murder, crime-of-passion sort of thing, don't you think?'

'Henry,' said Mr. Brockhurst firmly, 'go to bed.'

So it was just Clarence, his father, and I who sat in the living room waiting for the police to come. We didn't speak much. I think we were all in shock. Presently Bunny came into the room with a puzzled look on her face.

'I can't find Chan anywhere,' she announced. 'He seems to have vanished.'

We all looked at each other, letting the significance of this fact sink in, and then the doorbell rang. For a moment the Brockhursts all sat there, until they realized Chan wasn't going to answer the door, and Bunny jumped up and went into the hall.

A few seconds later we met Detective DaSilva of the San Mateo County Sheriff's Department. Detective DaSilva, a swarthy middle-aged man, strode into the library, removed his hat and flipped back his lapel, revealing a nickel-plated star. 'What seems to be the trouble?' he said.

'I'd better let you see for yourself,' said Mr. Brockhurst. 'Follow me, please.' I was dying to go with them, but I thought it would look pushy.

When the two men had left to see the body, Bunny rummaged around in a large desk and produced the decanters that had been out earlier. 'Anyone want a drink?' she said. 'I could use one after seeing that poor girl like that.' She shuddered.

'Can't you wait until the police have left?' said an exasperated Clarence. 'It is against the law, you know.'

'Oh, all right,' said Bunny sulkily.

'I suppose Chan did it,' I said. 'And then ran away. How tragic.'

'It does seem suspicious that he's gone,' admitted Bunny. 'But Chan doesn't seem the type to go off the deep end like that.'

Clarence's eyes narrowed. 'It's a mistake for us to imagine we can plumb the depths of the celestial mind,' he said ominously.

I hesitated. 'I *did* overhear that girl being rude to him,' I said reluctantly.

'There, you see?' said Clarence to Bunny. 'Probably strangled her in a cold rage.'

'She wasn't strangled,' I said.

'Maybe Chan used some untraceable Oriental poison,' said Bunny, her eyes opening wide.

'If it's true, Chan was very foolish to bolt,' I said. 'And he didn't strike me as a foolish man.'

Suddenly the doorbell rang again.

'More policemen?' said Bunny, raising her eyebrows.

'I'll get it this time,' said Clarence. He rose and went to the door.

From the hall I heard a familiar voice: 'Well, well, young Mr. Brockhurst, I guess. I'm Jack Clancy. Say, I heard you folks had some trouble up here tonight. I sure would appreciate knowing . . .'

Startled, I got up and ran into the hall. There was no mistaking that cheerful and persuasive voice. It was Jack Clancy all right, standing there framed by the door, Clarence looming in front of him.

'Jack!' I exclaimed. 'What are you doing here?'

'Iris! Iris Cooper!' Jack whipped off his hat and barreled past Clarence and came to greet me. He stopped just short of an embrace, then took my hand awkwardly. 'What are you

54

doing here?'

'I'm visiting the Brockhursts,' I began.

'So I heard, so I heard,' said Jack glibly. 'And I promised your aunt I'd look after you, so when I heard about your trouble I thought I'd come right up and see if everything were in apple-pie order.' He turned to Clarence. 'I'm an old friend of the family, see. You're taking good care of Miss Cooper, I trust.'

I was furious. Jack was full of outrageous lies. First of all, he hadn't known I was with the Brockhursts. He had just asked me what I was doing there! I hadn't seen him since the summer before when we had both sailed on the Irenia and solved a baffling mystery together. Second, my aunt had certainly not asked him to keep an eye on me. She had confidence that I could take care of myself quite nicely.

'Oh really, Jack,' I said rather angrily. In my initial delight at seeing him again I'd forgotten how cross I had been with him for not getting in touch with me when I'd arrived at Stanford. I turned to Clarence. 'You should know,' I said, 'that Jack—er, Mr. Clancy here—is a reporter for the San Francisco *Globe*.'

Bunny had joined us in the hall now. 'The *Globe*. How thrilling,' she said. 'I read it all the time, as soon as Cook is finished with it.' Jack irritated me by eyeing Bunny in her black pajamas appreciatively while I stumbled through some introductions.

'Well,' began Clarence, 'if Mr. Clancy is a friend of yours, Iris . . .'

'We simply sailed together last summer,' I said, trying to put a little ice in my voice. On the one hand I would have rather enjoyed having Clarence eject Jack Clancy. But on the other hand I was glad to see Jack again. After all, there was another mystery to solve, and Jack and I had worked so well together before.

'Oh, come on in and have a drink,' said Bunny hospitably. Clarence looked a little vexed.

'Well, thank you,' said Jack, strolling into the library and making himself annoyingly at home. He gazed around at some of the pictures. 'Got yourself a dead body, I hear. What a story.'

'Bunny,' hissed Clarence, 'Detective DaSilva will be back down any minute. Must you flaunt that whiskey decanter?'

Jack laughed heartily. 'DeSilva won't care. Why, it's practically common knowledge that his brothers and cousins are all rumrunners out of Half Moon Bay down the coast. Don't you worry about DaSilva.' He accepted a glass from Bunny and took a sip.

'Now tell me all about the body,' he said. 'Don't tell me Iris discovered it? She's making a habit of discovering bodies while in her pajamas.'

56

'Well, as a matter of fact, she did,' said Bunny brightly. 'Of course, Clarence was there too,' she added.

'That's right,' I said, a little defiantly. 'Clarence and I were upstairs with his mummy.'

'Well, I'm glad you were chaperoned. I guess that makes it all right for you two to be prowling around together in your pajamas,' said Jack, whipping out his pigskin-bound notebook. He sat there for a second with his pencil poised over the page. 'Now what was Mummy wearing? Our female readers appreciate the fashion notes.'

'Yards and yards of nasty-looking tattered strips,' I said, getting some satisfaction from Jack's startled face.

CHAPTER FIVE

Clarence scowled. 'It's nothing to joke about,' he said. 'Iris is referring to Ra-Hotep.'

Jack beamed. 'You mean like King Tut? Boy, what a story. The mummy's-curse angle.'

'You see,' I said patiently, 'the body was found in the mummy case. The mummy itself was nearby.'

'Sounds great,' said Jack. 'Girl slain as mummy watches. Silent witness to tragedy. If only the dead could speak. There are a lot of possibilities here.'

His musings were interrupted by the sound of heavy feet coming down the stairs. Followed by Mr. Brockhurst, Lieutenant DaSilva, now smoking a cigar, barked, 'Where's the phone?' and glanced into the library. 'Clancy? What are you doing here?'

'Don't you remember, Al? I was playing cards at the station house with some of the boys when the call came in.' He turned to us. 'And my editor thought he was punishing me by sending me down to cover the sleepy little peninsula. Wait till he hears about this!' He sprang up from the sofa. 'Hold on, DaSilva, let me use the phone first, will you? I gotta get Flash down here.'

'Flash?' said Bunny, eyebrows raised.

'I imagine he's referring to a photographer,' I said drily.

'Oh really?' said Bunny, her hand smoothing down her hair. 'How thrilling.'

'Not so fast,' said DaSilva. 'Police business comes first.' He eyed the decanter on the bar, and Bunny obliged him by pouring him a drink.

'Thanks. Appreciate it. I'd call this medicinal use. Not a pretty sight, not at all.' He shook his head.

'The phone's here in the hall,' said Mr. Brockhurst. 'Will this take long, Lieutenant? I was rather hoping you'd simply be able to remove the, er, corpse, and do whatever it is you have to do *elsewhere*.'

DaSilva gave him a withering look and drained his Scotch. 'It'll take as long as it takes, that's how long it'll take,' he said, and headed toward the phone. 'Hello, Central,' he bellowed into the instrument, while Jack swept me toward the stairs.

'Let's go take a look, Iris,' he said. 'Show me exactly how you discovered the body.'

'I was there, too,' said Clarence.

'Okay, okay,' said Jack, proceeding purposefully up the stairs. Bunny, who had screamed and practically swooned at her first sight of the corpse, was acting very blasé about it now and trooped along, drawn, I thought, partly by her interest in the colorful Jack, partly because she wouldn't want to be left out of his story in the *Globe*. My suspicions were confirmed when she remarked: 'Well, this is a lot different than that old stuffy society column. Won't the girls be just green?'

Lieutenant DaSilva started to bellow something in our direction, but Jack kept marching up, and we all followed.

'Pretty swell layout,' Jack remarked bluntly, as we proceeded up the wide, imposing staircase. 'Now tell me exactly what you're doing here, Iris.'

'I'm visiting,' I said.

'You a friend of Bunny here?' he inquired

dubiously. 'Travelling in a pretty fast set, aren't you?'

'Oh, really, Jack,' I said, exasperated, but Bunny just giggled. 'Iris is my brother Clarence's friend,' she said. 'Clarence hardly qualifies as one of the bright young things. They're both interested in old, dead things. Like that mummy.'

'I suppose the police will be stomping all through my room up there,' said Clarence sulkily. 'Why did the wretched girl have to go there to die?'

'I'm sure she didn't mean to,' I said rather tartly.

'Here we are,' said Clarence morosely, as we entered his sanctum.

'Isn't it too dreadful?' said Bunny.

Jack went inside and knelt by the body for a moment. We were all silent, and he said finally, and in a low voice, 'It sure is. A real damn shame.'

He rose and stepped back a pace, surveying the room. 'She fell out of that thing, I take it?'

'Ra-Hotep's coffin,' said Clarence. 'A remarkable example from the eighteenth dynasty.'

'Who was she?'

'He. He was a scribe,' said Clarence, misunderstanding.

'Her name was Florence Smith,' said Bunny. 'She was a lady's maid.'

'Mrs. Brockhurst's maid? Or yours?'

'Another guest's,' Bunny explained. 'Madame Sophie's.'

'Madame Sophie? Sounds like a dressmaker.'

'A medium,' I said.

'You mean a spiritualist?'

'That's right.'

'More and more interesting,' said Jack. 'I better call the *Globe* and tell them to reset page one. I wonder if DaSilva's off the phone?' He turned to go and then he said: 'But I don't know what I'll say yet. There isn't a mark on the body. I wonder what killed her?'

Lieutenant DaSilva had joined us now. 'Will you young people get out of here,' he said. 'And you, Clancy. Why, you newsboys are nothing but a bunch of ghouls.'

Jack ignored this. 'What killed her, Lieutenant?'

'Damned if I know. That's what the doc's supposed to tell us. But I don't like the looks of it, not one bit.'

He eyed me and the Brockhursts suspiciously.

'Well, thanks, DaSilva, you just wrote my lead.' Jack breezed off back down the stairs, and the rest of us followed. On the way down, Clarence took my arm. 'I'm surprised you know this fellow, Iris,' he began. 'He doesn't seem quite, well . . . .'

'Jack has terrible manners, I know,' I replied. 'But I'm sure he's very good at his job. I know he feels the same way about his work as you do about yours.'

Clarence snorted. 'Writing a lot of drivel for shopgirls and town loafers to read. It's just awful.'

Back downstairs, Jack was leaning against the wall, with the receiver of the telephone squeezed between shoulder and ear while he leaned in toward the speaking horn mounted on the wall. He was writing in his notebook as he spoke. 'Get me rewrite,' he said, his green eyes glittering.

'I don't know if Mother will want all this publicity,' began Clarence.

Jack turned to him. 'I think we should do a little sidebar on your Egyptian work,' he said smoothly. 'Now how do you spell the name of your dead friend up there? Ra-something, wasn't it?'

Clarence smiled. 'Ra-Hotep,' he began. He began to spell while Jack solemnly took it all down.

'What a fascinating friend you have,' said Bunny, giving me a sisterly squeeze on the arm. 'I never meet men like that. Just the usual old deb escorts.'

'Rewrite? Hi, Joe. Clancy here. Now get this and get it good. Quote "I don't like the looks of it one bit" close quote. "A grim detective Alphonse DaSilva of the San Mateo

62

County police was ashen-faced at the sight of a beautiful, scantily clad blonde corpse, found inside the thousand-year-old mummy case . . ."'

'Three thousand, three thousand,' interrupted Clarence, waving his hands. 'At least three thousand.'

'Make that "*ancient* mummy case, in the palatial Hillsborough mansion of city businessman and social leader, Mr. Edgar Brockhurst. Our reporter was on the scene in the small hours of the morning soon after the grisly discovery was made by young Clarence Brockhurst and his pretty young fiancée."' He looked over at me. 'Say, are you engaged to this fellow, Iris?'

'No,' I said firmly.

'Kill "fiancée." Make that "a pretty young co-ed, Iris Cooper. Also present at the scene was vivacious society beauty and daughter of the house, Miss Bunny Brockhurst."'

'You can tell him the butler probably did it,' said Bunny, getting into the spirit of things.

'The butler? Hang on, Joe. The details are coming fast and furious. What's this about the butler?'

'He's missing,' I said.

'Move that stuff about the debutante down,' said Jack, rather to my satisfaction. 'Get this. The butler is missing.' He turned to us. 'What's his name?'

'Chan,' said Bunny.

'What's his first name?'

'I think it's Charles,' said Clarence.

'Charlie Chan? What a story,' gloated Jack. 'Got that?' said Jack. 'Now, for heaven's sake, get Flash down here . . .' He turned to the Brockhursts. 'What's the address?'

Bunny supplied it eagerly.

The Brockhursts seemed helpful to the point of naïveté. Aunt Hermione had always told me that no matter what had transpired, the newspapers could always make you look very foolish, so it was best to try and stick to the old dictum about a lady's name appearing in the paper only when she was born, married, and died.

'And listen to this, Joe,' said Jack. 'The mummy was right there, next to the girl, and the victim was wearing step-ins and a camisole thing . . . kind of pinkish.'

Jack was falling down a bit in this part of his narrative.

'In peach silk with a wide border of Valenciennes lace,' I lied sweetly.

'Great, great,' said Jack, repeating what I'd said. 'No, I don't know how you spell Valenciennes. Look it up.'

It seemed rather odd, really, that she had such lovely underthings. Much more expensive than you would expect. But then, there was a lot to learn about Florence, I imagined.

64

We heard the arrival of some men at the door.

'Listen, I got to go, Joe, here's the doctor now. No, I don't know what killed her, but I think we can say she was killed. We have that quote from DaSilva. Just say "foul play is feared in the bizarre death of blah, blah, blah." Victim's name is Florence Smith. I'll call you back. So long.'

He hung up, satisfied. 'That'll blast Mayor Rolph off of page one,' he said, rubbing his hands together.

Lieutenant DaSilva and Mr. Brockhurst, now smoking nervously, had gone to the door and let in a batch of blue-coated policemen and a stout little man in a dark coat and hat, carrying a doctor's kit. They all clomped upstairs, and Jack followed them.

'Okay,' DaSilva was saying, 'follow me up here, this way, Doc. You men start looking for the butler Chan. He didn't have a gas buggy, they tell me, so he can't have gone far.' In answer to a question from one of the officers, he snapped, 'What do you mean, what does he look like? He looks Oriental, of course.'

I thought it would be pressing things if I accompanied the doctor upstairs. So I went back into the library with Clarence and settled into a corner of the sofa.

'Let's all go back to bed,' said Clarence.

'Not on your life,' said Bunny. 'This is all

too thrilling.'

I couldn't help but agree with her. I, for one, was staying right where I was until I heard from the doctor what had apparently killed poor Florence, and I said so.

'Well, I'll stay here with you then,' said Clarence. 'In any case, I'll want to have a look at my artifacts after the police have been there and taken out that girl.'

'Do you think I should change for the photographer?' mused Bunny. 'Maybe a nice morning frock?'

'Well, I would think at least a bathrobe,' I said, glancing at her pajamas. 'Which reminds me,' I continued. 'Did you notice her clothes, Bunny?'

'Not much clothes at all, I'd say,' remarked Clarence.

'Really lovely, weren't they?' said Bunny.

'Well,' I said slowly, 'I don't know how much Madame Sophie paid her, but I can't imagine Florence would have been able to afford such elegant things on her wages.'

'I imagine you're right,' said Bunny. 'I suppose maids usually wear some sensible cotton things.' She narrowed her eyes. 'There must have been a *man* in the picture. You know, some old lecher buying her fancy little scanties.'

'Oh *really*, Bunny,' said Clarence. 'Is that all you can think of?'

'*Cherchez l'homme*,' said Bunny, yawning

and stretching her arms above her head. 'Too bad Chan has bolted. What I wouldn't give for a cup of coffee right now.'

'Let's go make some,' I suggested. 'The policemen might like some too.'

'Oh, what a good idea,' said Bunny. 'Do you know how?'

Frankly, I had suggested making coffee mainly to give myself something to do. I hate being inactive in an emergency. How I envied Jack, upstairs with the police learning more about the mystery.

It took us a while, but Bunny and I managed to find everything we needed, as well as a tin of cookies. We made the coffee, arranged everything on a large tray, and carried it all back toward the library.

In the hall we saw Lieutenant DaSilva saying goodbye to the doctor at the door. Jack Clancy was back at the phone, leaning against the wall and dictating into the receiver.

'Okay, listen, now. "The slain beauty's death is at present a medical mystery. Our reporter on the scene at the coroner's preliminary examination has learned that there is no apparent cause of death. Was she murdered? And was she murdered, not by an ordinary killer, but by a curse reaching thousands of years into the future from beneath the shifting sands above a pharaoh's final resting place? Was it a curse so powerful it could snuff out a bright young life like an evil wind blowing out a dancing flame? The only witness is mute, the ancient, preserved Egyptian mummy, whose grinning skull leered out over the awful scene in cruel mockery." Got that? Clean it up and run it in the morning edition. I'll have more later.'

He replaced the receiver and, looking slightly exhausted from his literary exertions, he smiled at us. 'Swell. Coffee. Just what I need. Let me help you with that tray.'

'So they don't know yet what killed her, Jack?' I said, as we made our way into the library.

'Nope. Unless she had a heart attack from being shut up inside that mummy case. The sight of the mummy himself could have finished *me* off, I tell you.' Jack shuddered.

'I heard that,' said Clarence, from over by the fireplace.

'Didn't mean to be casting aspersions on your dear old mummy,' said Jack good-naturedly.

'But what would Florence be doing closed up in a mummy case in step-ins and a vest in the first place?' mused Bunny.

'Who knows?' replied Jack. 'Wild houseparty. Youthful hijinks. Collegiate capers. Madcap debutante. I'll pursue that angle in my next story maybe.'

I rolled my eyes heavenward and Bunny giggled.

'Really, Mr. Clancy,' said Clarence

68

indignantly.

'Well,' said Jack, sipping his coffee, 'just what *were* you and Miss Cooper doing up there in the middle of the night, anyway? In pajamas, I might add. My readers may want to know.'

Lieutenant DaSilva came into the room. 'I've sent your father upstairs to wake the rest of the household. I'm sorry, but it must be done. We need to know more about this business.'

'We sure do,' said Jack.

'And we can throw Mr. Clancy out any time you want,' added the lieutenant, advancing on Jack with a gleam in his eye.

'Fine,' said Clarence.

I really could see Clarence's point. If the lurid prose I'd overheard in the hall was any indication, not to mention hints at wild houseparties and that kind of thing, there was really nothing to be gained by the affair being ventilated in the *Globe*.

'I can't leave now,' said Jack. 'Not before I get my story. The real story. The story behind the story. The story of young Egyptologist Clarence Brockhurst and his mummy. You have quite a collection of treasures up there, I noticed. I'm sure my readers will be fascinated.'

'Well, it is a fascinating business, I admit,' said Clarence. 'And the public is sadly misinformed about the field. All this mummy's-curse nonsense, for instance.'

Jack didn't even flinch at this last remark, which was pretty cool, I thought, considering he'd just telephoned in a story about the mummy's curse that would have made Rider Haggard blush.

'Well,' he said, 'was there a curse on that tomb?'

'Oh, just a little one,' said Clarence. 'Very common at that time. Superstitious nonsense, of course.'

Just then we heard a bloodcurdling scream from the hall. I rushed out to see what had happened. Bunny, Clarence, and Jack followed.

Here we were presented with a vivid tableau. On the stairs, standing silently, were grouped the members of the household and Lieutenant DaSilva. Henry, Aunt Laura, the Grand Duke Boris, Mr. Leonard. Mr. Brockhurst brought up the rear. Ahead of them were Mrs. Brockhurst and Mr. Jones, flanking a shrieking Madame Sophie who had half collapsed against them. Below her, two policemen were carrying a stretcher draped with a white sheet obviously covering the body of Florence.

'Oh, it's terrible,' shrieked Madame Sophie. 'I knew it would happen. The curse. I warned you, but no one listened.'

'There she goes, off on that curse business again,' said Clarence.

'Couldn't you have taken the body down the servants' stairs?' demanded Mrs. Brockhurst of the police. 'You've upset Madame Sophie.'

I remembered the little maid sauntering down the steps earlier that evening, and thought that she would have preferred not to be taken down the servants' stairs.

Mr. Jones tried to soothe his employer, and the lieutenant waved at the policemen to get on with the job. Just then the door flew open and a huge flash of light burst out through the darkness, lighting up the entire group and throwing sparks into the air.

One of the policemen, obviously startled, let go of his end of the stretcher, and the corpse slid down a little from beneath the sheet. For a hideous moment we all stared at Florence's exposed calves and feet. The policeman twitched the sheet back over her feet and the two men continued through the hall and out of the door.

Jack hailed a thin, dour-looking man in a snap-brim hat who stood at the door, camera in hand.

'Flash!' Jack cried. 'That should be a swell picture. Come on in.'

Something about Florence's feet had surprised me. I was puzzled for a moment, and then it came to me. There was a reddish mark, a strange wavy pattern on her calf. And then I noticed the feet and their pink soles.

71

There wasn't a speck of dust on them.

When Clarence and I had made our way up to the mummy room, I had noticed that the attic needed a good turning out. In fact, Clarence's mother had said earlier that the servants refused to dust up in that part of the house. However Florence had arrived at her final resting place, it hadn't been on foot. Unless, of course, she'd lost a pair of shoes and stockings along the way.

CHAPTER SIX

I was suddenly very tired. It had been hours since Clarence and I had discovered the body, and I was keyed up and wide awake, but exhausted nevertheless.

Lieutenant DaSilva was arranging us in the library and explained that he would be asking us to come one by one into the hall where he would ask us some simple questions. Apparently he had already roused the poor servants and grilled them.

DaSilva talked to Clarence first, then me, spending just a few minutes with each of us. He asked me if I knew the girl, and I told him I'd just seen her once. Reluctantly, because I had sympathized so with Chan, I mentioned that the girl had been unpleasant to him. 'We'll find him,' he said confidently.

'I suppose there's no question he killed her?' I said.

'Not a doubt in my mind.'

'But is there any proof she *was* killed?'

The policeman waved his hand in the air impatiently. 'The doctor's working on that now. Who knows? Maybe it was some untraceable poison from the mysterious East.' Then, pulling back as if he'd told me too much, he said, 'Send in Miss Brockhurst, will you?'

'Which one?' I said. 'Bunny or Aunt Laura?'

'Oh, that's right. There are two. Well, send in the girl first.'

I returned to the library and Bunny went out. Jack was holding forth to Mrs. Brockhurst, who seemed most attentive.

'In short,' he said, 'I think you'll find it a real help to have someone with a knowledge of the newspaper business around here to help you fend off the press. Let me tell you, the gentlemen of the press are, upon occasion, I am very sorry to say, not gentlemen.'

'Well, that sounds like a good idea,' said Mrs. Brockhurst. 'And I'm sure you have many interesting stories to tell about the newspaper business, Mr. Clancy.'

Mr. Brockhurst drew his brows together. 'Perhaps, dear,' he said to his wife, 'we'd better discuss this later. We're all distraught

73

and can't make a wise decision right now . . .'

But Mrs. Brockhurst seemed charmed by Jack, just as she had presumably been charmed by the Grand Duke Boris and by Madame Sophie and Mr. Jones. Poor Mr. Brockhurst had, no doubt, a vision of a new and possibly permanent guest.

Clarence intervened. 'You know, Father, it really isn't such a bad idea. And if Mr. Clancy is around the house for a few days until this all blows over, why I can make sure he gets all the details correct. He'll be doing a story on my expedition and the discoveries I've made.'

Bunny returned shortly and Jack was called out into the hall.

'And Mr. Clancy tells me he's a friend of Iris's family,' continued Mrs. Brockhurst, the conversation, because of our comings and goings, becoming a strange sort of round robin. 'Why not let him stay a few days? He may be right. The press may well descend on us *en masse*.'

It was obvious to me that Jack wanted to get an exclusive story for the *Globe* and do some sleuthing around on his own. Maybe I could join him. That would be thrilling. But I really didn't want Jack around just when Clarence and I were—well, I could foresee an awkward situation. Neither did I like the idea of the Brockhursts being victimized by Jack's brand of journalism. Most irritating of all, he had used my connection with him as an entrée to the house. It was all too confusing. But it was my clear duty to delicately warn the family about Jack's motives.

'Mr. Clancy,' I said a little stiffly, 'is a reporter himself. He's already phoned in several stories to his newspaper.'

'How did you meet such an interesting man?' said Mrs. Brockhurst. 'I do love interesting people.'

'We sailed aboard the same ship,' I replied.

'Seems like a real go-getter,' said Mr. Leonard, with approval. 'Right on top of that story, wasn't he? Nice to see a young man with that fighting competitive spirit.'

'I see no need to take him into the bosom of the family on that basis,' said Mr. Brockhurst.

'I think he's sweet,' said Bunny.

'He seems genuinely interested in my work,' added Clarence.

'Well, he's been up all night, poor boy. We must at least ask him to stay to breakfast. And then maybe he'd like a little nap or something. We've all been through so much, haven't we?' said Mrs. Brockhurst. She went over to Madame Sophie, who seemed to be snuffling into a handkerchief, with the attentive Mr. Jones at her side.

'Are you feeling stronger, dear?' Mrs. Brockhurst asked. 'We won't let that policeman ask you any questions until you feel stronger. I'll explain to him about your delicate vibrations.'

'They'll be anxious to ask Madame Sophie about Florence,' I said. 'Where she was engaged and so forth. I don't imagine they know much about her.' Perhaps Madame Sophie would tell us something about the dead girl.

Mr. Jones spoke up. 'We really don't know much about her, either, do we? Florence was a quiet girl. Kept to herself a good deal.'

I didn't believe this for a moment. My brief impression of Florence had been quite different.

'Of course,' added Mr. Jones, 'Madame Sophie is terribly distraught. After all, something very terrible has happened.'

'Must have had some kind of a fit and died or something,' said Mr. Leonard.

'The doctor doesn't seem to know what happened to her,' I replied.

'Well, maybe she did have a fit or something,' said young Henry. 'But where's Chan? The mathematical odds against her dying of a fit in that mummy case and Chan disappearing at the same time are probably pretty high.' He looked for a moment as if he meant to calculate them.

Jack popped his head into the room and summoned Aunt Laura, then announced that he and Flash had received permission from the police to go up and photograph Clarence's mummy room. 'I told him it was okay with you folks,' he added, then disappeared.

'That man is going to be a real nuisance,' Mr. Brockhurst said irritably to his wife. 'And you want to invite him to stay. He'll be like that swami you had here for a year and a half. He was a real nuisance, and the servants hated him.'

'Well, I can't imagine Mr. Clancy will insist on a vegetarian diet,' said Mrs. Brockhurst. 'I'll ask him.'

Lieutenant DaSilva was true to his word and spent very little time with each of us. We all compared notes about his questions, which seemed to be all the same. Had we known Florence well? When was she last seen? And so forth. He also asked some questions about Chan, but the Brockhursts knew astonishingly little about him too. He had come with references from a professor who was at present on an expedition in the Amazon, and from an old lady who had died. The Brockhursts hadn't bothered to check further.

'But he was such a wonderful butler,' said Grand Duke Boris expansively, as Chan was being discussed. 'Like all truly excellent servants, he had the mark of the born aristocrat about him.'

'Yes, it is hard to believe he could have done anything to poor Florence,' agreed Mrs.

Brockhurst. 'Things have run so smoothly since he's been here.' She sighed. 'They must let us keep him.'

'Well,' I said, 'I don't see how they can charge him with murder unless there is evidence of a murder. So far they don't know what killed Florence.'

'Ah,' said Madame Sophie. 'Not everything on our plane can be explained, without taking into account the forces that work on our lives from the other side.'

'Are you saying supernatural forces killed her?' demanded Henry. 'Ridiculous.'

'Oh, look,' said Bunny, going to the French doors. 'It's morning. We've been up all night.'

'What will we do about breakfast?' said Mrs. Brockhurst fretfully. 'How annoying of Chan to have disappeared like that.'

'I hope nothing untoward happened to him,' said Aunt Laura, who had quietly returned.

'I hadn't thought of that,' said Madame Sophie. 'Perhaps the curse has struck again.'

'Oh, really,' said Mr. Brockhurst.

'It's all so bothersome,' said Mrs. Brockhurst. 'Laura, dear, do you think you could make some kind of arrangements in the kitchen? Make sure Cook isn't upset. And maybe Betty can serve. She's only a housemaid, but I'm sure she can manage.'

'All right,' said Aunt Laura dutifully, and

rose to leave. But before she reached the door, Chan stepped into the room from the servants' hall. He was carrying a newspaper.

'I didn't find you in your room, Mr. Brockhurst,' he said. 'Betty told me you were here, so I thought it best to bring the newspaper here. Would you also like your coffee in here?' He glanced around the room with a flicker of curiosity, confused by our presence.

'Chan! Where have you been?' said Mr. Brockhurst. 'The police are looking for you.'

'The police?' Chan showed another flicker of emotion, but it had almost a trace of amusement in it.

'Yes. A girl was found dead here last night. Florence Smith, Madame Sophie's maid.'

Chan looked genuinely surprised this time. He let the newspaper drop to the floor. It was then I noticed that the apparently perfect butler had made a little mistake. He had offered the newspaper to Mr. Brockhurst with his bare hands. The silver salver I'd seen him carrying before wasn't there. Chan, despite his casual entrance, was definitely off his form.

'I see,' said Chan.

Mr. Leonard, who had been outside being interviewed, came back into the room. 'Why, it's the butler,' he exclaimed, and DaSilva followed close on his heels.

'So it is,' snarled DaSilva. 'I think we'll ask

79

him his questions down at the station house.'

'Can't this wait until after breakfast?' said Mrs. Brockhurst.

'Are you charging him with anything?' demanded her husband.

'No. Not till we hear from the doctor. But he left the house. That's mighty suspicious.'

'But he came back, didn't he?' said Aunt Laura simply.

'That's true,' acknowledged DaSilva.

'It will be devastating to our domestic arrangements to have Chan taken away. He's an absolute treasure,' said Mrs. Brockhurst.

'Believe me, we've had plenty of servant problems,' chimed in Bunny.

'Well, if you're willing to put up with a killer to solve your servant problems,' sputtered the policeman, 'well then . . .'

'But he didn't kill anyone. Not that we know of,' persisted Mrs. Brockhurst. 'I mean, we don't *know* that Florence was killed, do we?'

'Let me handle this,' said Lieutenant DaSilva, and he hustled Chan out into the hall. 'For now I'll just ask him where he's been.'

Aunt Laura looked thoughtful. 'I wonder too,' she said.

'Wonder what, Aunt Laura?' said Clarence vaguely.

'Where he's been,' she replied.

'Oh, probably an *affaire de coeur*,' said

Grand Duke Boris. 'If Chan is the gentleman I think he is, he won't give away the lady's name.' He stroked his moustache in a man-of-the-world way.

'Boris,' said Aunt Laura gently, with a little blush.

A few minutes later, Lieutenant DaSilva came back into the library. 'Can't get it out of him,' he fumed.

'There, you see,' said the grand duke with a gesture of triumph.

'I suppose it isn't really correct for one's butler to go prowling around at night,' said Mrs. Brockhurst dubiously.

'Even servants have their own needs,' said Boris. I wondered if he were thinking of his years as a major-domo or whatever he had been. His interest in and sympathy for Chan was understandable. I wondered if he would have been so sympathetic to the serving class before the revolution put the grand duke himself in their ranks.

'I don't care what he does, as long as I get the paper and my coffee brought to my room at seven as usual, and three squares a day properly served, and an efficient household. Which, I might add, has been a new and delightful experience for this family,' said Mr. Brockhurst.

'Not to mention the hooch,' added Bunny. 'Chan's done nicely by us there.' Clarence gestured to her to abandon this line in front of

81

DaSilva, but she just made a face at her brother.

'Well, if you want him around, I guess that's all right. At least until we hear from the doctor. But I wish I could get him down to the station house. I'd get him to talk there.' DaSilva looked grim.

Jack walked into the room. 'Same old tactics, eh, DaSilva? Or maybe bamboo under the fingernails for Chan?'

'Oh, how horrid,' said Mrs. Brockhurst. She turned to her husband. 'Edgar, don't let this man take Chan away.'

Mr. Brockhurst stroked his chin. 'Well, we could arrange for a lawyer for him.'

'Save your breath,' said DaSilva. 'He's already got one. Up in the city. A white lawyer, too. He's a pretty cool customer.'

Chan came back into the room. 'As everyone is up,' he said, 'I took the liberty of deciding to serve breakfast at an earlier hour. I hope you agree, madame. Things are a little,' he coughed delicately, 'irregular this morning.'

'That would be fine, Chan,' said Mrs. Brockhurst.

'Coffee is served in the dining room then,' he said, 'and breakfast will follow shortly. How many will there be, madame?'

'There will be a few extra people,' said Mrs. Brockhurst, looking around. 'Mr. Clancy, you are staying, aren't you? And

82

perhaps Mr., er, Flash?'

'He's already on his way back to the city with pictures,' said Jack, 'but I'd be delighted to stay. You're very kind.'

Chan turned to the policeman. 'And will Lieutenant DaSilva be staying?'

'No. I have to get back,' snarled the policeman.

As we trooped into the dining room, Jack said to me, 'That first edition has been out about an hour now. We can expect the rest of the press to descend on us at any time. Boy, I scooped the town. And by the time they get their stories in, the *Globe* will have pictures.' He looked terribly pleased with himself.

In the hall Chan was handing Lieutenant DaSilva his hat with a solemn face. In the dining room we were startled to see him making a few last-minute touches to the table.

'Didn't we just leave Chan in the hall?' asked Jack, surprised to see him.

'Oh, he whisked back through the servants' passage,' said Bunny. 'Chan's very fast and light on his feet.'

As I watched the butler moving across the carpet with a silver coffee pot, I reflected that Lieutenant DaSilva was right. Chan was indeed a very cool customer.

He served an excellent breakfast, and we spoke little. I, for one, thought it imprudent to discuss the case in front of Chan until we knew more.

83

The soft murmurs of desultory conversation and the clink of silver and china were interrupted by a sudden commotion outside. Automobiles seemed to be pulling up in front of the house, masculine voices were heard, and there was a pounding on the door. Chan went into the hall. A little later we heard the door slam, and Chan returned again. He spoke to Mrs. Brockhurst.

'The press are here,' he announced. 'There are quite a few of them and they are trampling the rose gardens. They opened the gates themselves and drove right in. What do you wish me to do?'

Jack threw his napkin down. 'I'll take care of them for you,' he said. 'I'll issue a simple statement and tell them to clear out.'

'That does seem wise,' said Mr. Brockhurst. 'Of course I could do that myself.'

'Better leave it to me,' said Jack. 'I know these boys.'

I strained to hear him from the hall. There was a lot of noise and yelling, and even some scuffling sounds. Finally, I heard Jack's voice raised above the din. 'If you want to know about it, just read the *Globe*, boys. Warm over my stuff. It won't be the first time, will it? Ha! Now just clear out, or we'll have the police do it for us. The Brockhursts don't want to be disturbed. And get your big feet out of the garden beds.'

He came back into the dining room with a triumphant smirk.

'Is it really fair to treat your colleagues that way?' said Aunt Laura.

'Fair? Of course not. But who ever said this business was fair?' replied Jack.

'Really,' said Mr. Leonard to Mr. Brockhurst, giving Jack a rather dubious look, 'it might make it easier for us to get on with our business if this young fellow manages to keep the peace somehow. After all, this will probably blow over in a few days when the doctor comes up with his verdict. Meanwhile you can be spared having to deal with that mob out there.'

'Oh, all right,' said Mr. Brockhurst gloomily, looking at Jack with a frown.

'You aren't a vegetarian, are you, Mr. Clancy?' said Mrs. Brockhurst with a smile, as Jack dove into his bacon.

CHAPTER SEVEN

After breakfast Clarence wanted me to go upstairs with him and work on the pottery shards, but I declined. I said I was going to my room and take a nap. After all, I had been up half the night. Quite a lot had happened during those hours. Clarence had practically asked me to become engaged. We had discovered poor Florence's body. Madame Sophie had gone nearly berserk with grief or fear or superstition, I wasn't sure which. The police had quizzed us all, and I had had to tell them Clarence and I were going up to the attic to look at Egyptian artifacts at practically two in the morning, which I'm sure sounded a bit thin, though it was true. And Jack Clancy had breezed in and taken over the Brockhurst household by sheer force of personality, throwing me into an uneasy state, as I wasn't sure how I felt about him, and I was there to ascertain how I felt about Clarence. Even more annoying, Jack seemed so preoccupied with getting a story, he'd barely exchanged two words with me, which made me feel miffed even though I wasn't sure I wanted him around in the first place. It was all too confusing.

Of course I didn't sleep a wink. I lay on my bed thinking about how Florence got into that mummy case and what had killed her. And wondering about Chan and his mysterious reappearance, which was almost more peculiar than his disappearance, and which made me think he didn't know anything about Florence. I was just ruminating on how Florence could have been carried upstairs, because her smooth pink feet convinced me she hadn't walked, when there was a tap at my door.

I expected Clarence, pestering me about

those shards again, but it was Jack.

'Hello,' he said. 'You weren't really asleep, were you?'

'Well, I was just drifting off,' I began with a frown.

'Oh nonsense. When there's a mystery to be solved? That is not the Iris Cooper I remember. Now listen, I need you to help me. I want to get a good idea of the layout of this place.'

'Haven't you been given free rein already?' I said. 'You certainly seem to have made yourself at home.'

'No, not just the arrangement of the rooms,' said Jack, sauntering into the room and settling himself into a chair. 'I want to know more about the family.'

'Really, Jack, I'm a guest here. I can't tell you all about the Brockhursts for your paper.'

'Why not? What have they got to hide?'

'Nothing that I know about,' I said. 'It's just, well, I don't think it's right.'

'Tell me about this Clarence, for instance. You think he's stable? Think he's the kind to kill some cute little blonde, peel off her clothes and stuff her in that box? He seems awfully obsessed with mummies. Maybe he was going to work on a fresh one.'

'*Jack.* What a horrible thing to say! Clarence would never do anything like that. And I was there when he discovered the body. He was obviously surprised. Besides,' I said, 'we still don't know the girl was killed.'

'I just got the coroner's report over the phone,' said Jack.

'You did? How was she killed?' I demanded.

'You see. You *do* think she was killed. Doctor says she had a heart attack.'

'Well, I guess that's the end of the story,' I said. 'Of course it leaves a lot unanswered.'

'It certainly does,' said Jack. 'Like what was she doing up there.'

'I'm sure she was carried,' I said.

He leaned forward. 'How come?'

I explained to him about the girl's feet, free of dust, and the dusty stairs and floor of Clarence's little room.

'She was dead and she was moved. Very interesting. Now how could that happen? Wouldn't it look obvious, carrying a dead body around?'

'Oh, I don't know. There's a servants' passage all along the first floor. Chan seems to pop in and out of the wall because the passage opens in the library, the hall, and the dining room. And ends in the kitchen. Bunny showed it to me when we made coffee.'

'But presumably there are servants creeping around besides Chan,' said Jack. 'Anyway, that doesn't explain how she was carried upstairs. Or when. Exactly what happened here last night, and when did you see the maid last?'

'I only saw her once, actually.' I told him about Florence and her brief encounter with Chan on the main stairs.

'Interesting. No back passages for Florence, eh? Well, she sounds like a troublemaker. The servants all say so.'

'Have you talked to them?'

'Sure. They say she was always putting on airs. Expected them to wait on her. Which they didn't. And she didn't like the old lady she worked for much, but mostly she hated that Mr. Jones.'

'Why did she hate him?'

'No one knew. But I've got my suspicions. In my experience, there's usually only one thing that will bring out real hate between a man and a woman.'

I imagined he was speaking of passion, which reminded me that Bunny's lip rouge had appeared on Mr. Jones's collar last night at dinner. I told him about that.

'Are you sure?'

'Positive. Hardly anyone wears that absolutely crimson shade she wears.'

'A lively little thing, isn't she?' said Jack thoughtfully.

I started to tell him about the Brockhursts' dismissing their last chauffeur because of Bunny, but I thought better of it.

'Of course that Madame Sophie is probably a complete fake,' he said.

'Oh probably. Although she seems to have

89

taken in Mrs. B.' I told him about the previous night's séance.

'And you say everyone was there, except the servants? That would have been a good time for Chan to kill the girl and cart her away. Then leave the premises and then change his mind and come back.'

'But Chan was around after the séance. He came in with candles and so forth, and then Mr. Brockhurst said he could turn in. Madame Sophie and Mr. Jones went up next. Madame Sophie was complaining about the mummy's curse.'

'We'll have to find out if Madame Sophie saw the maid when she went up,' said Jack. 'I imagine DaSilva got at least that much out of her.'

'Didn't you corner her and badger her?' I asked.

'No. She went back to bed and stayed there. She's acting pretty cut up about the whole business.'

'Anyway, I was the next to go upstairs. Clarence followed me.'

'He did, huh.'

I blushed. 'Yes, he wanted me to help him sort out shards.'

'Shards?'

'Broken bits of pottery. From the tomb.'

'Sure he did. Tried pretty hard to get you up in that mummy room, didn't he? Finally broke you down later, in the middle of the

90

night.'

'Oh, really, Jack,' I said, annoyed.

'I thought these college boys liked to get girls out in canoes with ukuleles. Clarence is an original, all right. Well, never mind about that. I'm glad you're having a good time down on the Stanford Farm.'

'Clarence is very serious about those shards,' I said, remembering his persistence on the stairs. That brought back another memory. I had lurched into Clarence's arms when that dumbwaiter creaked.

'There's a dumbwaiter in this house,' I said. 'Maybe that's how someone got her up there. I heard it creak last night. When I was going upstairs.'

'But that was after the servants went off duty,' said Jack.

'That's right!'

'Let's take a look at it.' Jack sprang up.

I wasn't sure where it ended up, but I went out into the hall, and soon we found a little door in the wall that ended at waist height. 'This must be it,' I said, and we opened the door.

'You know what I'm thinking?' said Jack, as he peered into the shaft. 'I'm thinking maybe Florence was being pulled up to the attic in this thing while you were there on the stairs fending off Clarence and his shards.'

'That leaves Clarence out of it then,' I replied.

Jack pulled the ropes and a heavy counterweight inched by, followed soon by the box that was used to move things up and down the shaft.

'Look at that. It was up there in the attic, all right. Where does this thing come out?'

'Let's go up into the attic and see,' I said.

Jack took me by the elbow. 'No, let's go downstairs and see where they could have loaded it. Clarence is up there and we wouldn't want to disturb him while he's sorting shards, would we?'

'I suppose not,' I said, and we practically raced down the stairs and discovered another dumbwaiter door in a little pantry off the kitchen.

Jack peered down into the shaft. 'Someone could have put her in here, or down one more floor,' he said.

We explored until we found a basement door and went down there. The dumbwaiter ended, quite logically, in the laundry room. It was hot and steamy. There were sliding racks of wet sheets arranged in a row, with heating pipes.

Jack looked at these with interest. 'Why don't they just hang them out on the line?' he demanded.

'The Brockhursts are very correct,' I told him. 'I suppose they feel it's *déclassé* to have laundry hanging outside.' This sounded a little snobbish, so I added, 'At home we

92

always hang the laundry out on the line when the weather is fine. Aunt Hermione says it's much more hygienic. The sunlight—'

'Never mind about the laundry,' said Jack, 'here's the dumbwaiter door again.' He opened it up and peered inside. 'There's the big gear that runs the whole thing. Think it's stout enough to carry a body up to the attic? Let's give it a try.'

He began pulling on the ropes and, as he did, the big gear turned. A moment later we both saw a flutter of white fabric caught in the teeth of it.

'Well, what's this?' said Jack, retrieving a man's handkerchief. It was excellent quality, heavy linen, but there was no monogram. 'Interesting,' said Jack. 'Maybe it's a clue.' He put it in his pocket.

'Or maybe it fell in when they were sending the laundry up or down,' I replied. 'It could be anyone's. Although I suppose we should show it to the police.'

'Not a chance,' said Jack confidently. 'I'm going to crack this case myself. That DaSilva won't come up with anything. Why, look at that old horse doctor he had up here to look at the body. He can't even find out what killed the girl.' Jack was pulling on the ropes.

'Besides,' I said, 'you want this for the *Globe*.'

'That's right. Here it comes.' He was referring to the wooden box within the dumbwaiter shaft. 'Well, hop in.'

'What?'

'I want to see if it'll hold a body. You're about the same size as that girl. A little heavier maybe.'

'All right,' I said. 'But don't send me all the way up to the attic.'

I went into the dumbwaiter. It was very dark, but there was plenty of room in the thing. Jack began pulling and I rose jerkily. As soon as the thing made its way past the basement opening I was plunged into darkness. Jack cranked me up a little higher, and above me I saw a gleam of light around the door that opened out onto the pantry.

I heard voices above me and I was terrified that whoever was speaking would hear the creak of the rope. I was silent, wishing Jack would pull me back down again. As I rose slowly, I could make out the voices. They were unfamiliar to me. I imagined they must be servants, as they were speaking in the pantry.

'So he says, "Madame, I know it is my usual night off, and perhaps . . ." and Mrs. Brockhurst just says, nice as you please, "Oh, Chan, please take off on your usual night out." Not a word about where he went to last night.'

'They don't care what he does, as long as they're comfortable,' replied the other one. 'And he keeps Bunny in gin.'

94

Jack began cranking me back down at that point, thank goodness. What would I have done if they had opened the dumbwaiter door and seen me crouching there?

When I emerged back in the laundry room, I told Jack that I had overheard the maids talking. 'Apparently Chan is taking his usual night out tonight,' I said, brushing myself off.

Jack looked admiringly into the dumbwaiter. 'Gee,' he said, 'a fellow could find out a lot using one of these things. Well, what do you think, Iris, should we follow him?'

'Follow Chan?'

'Sure. On his night out. There's something pretty mysterious about that butler. I'd like to know what he does in his spare time. It's worth a try. Ever done any shadowing before?'

'Not really,' I said. It sounded like a thrilling idea.

'I'll find out when he gets off and I'll let you know,' said Jack. 'I'd better get on that right now.'

We parted, and Jack set off for the servants' hall, where he had apparently ingratiated himself as effectively as he had with the family.

Restless and bored, I decided to go help Clarence with the shards. We actually passed a rather pleasant afternoon up there among his artifacts. Poor Clarence, the police had moved everything around, and he had to sort bits and pieces all over again. I admired him so for his patience with the demanding work. And he was so pleased when I volunteered to help him. I felt rather guilty that I had ignored him since the body had been found, and I decided that it would probably be better if I didn't go off with Jack to shadow Chan later that evening. It really wasn't fair to Clarence. And I didn't want to have Clarence along. I suspected that he and Jack just wouldn't get along.

I had made up my mind to bow out of the adventure, when Jack sidled up to me at cocktails. 'Chan gets off right after dinner,' he said out of the side of his mouth. 'Usually his cousin picks him up in a car outside the servants' entrance. I've got my machine ready to follow, so be ready to leave right after dinner. Don't spread it around.'

At dinner Mrs. Brockhurst complained about the press. They had trampled the rose garden and put out cigarettes all over the terrace, she said. 'And then they all trooped down to the pool and took pictures of the house. It's really dreadful.'

'I thought Mr. Clancy was supposed to fend them off,' said Mr. Leonard.

'I kept them out of the house, didn't I?' said Jack. 'I went out there and gave them a few tidbits this afternoon and convinced them there wasn't much of a story up here. They all chased down to the sheriff's office to wait for the coroner's report.'

'Well, you've been very helpful, Mr. Clancy, I'm sure,' said Mr. Brockhurst. 'But now I imagine we can let you go back to your own home. Do stay for coffee, though.'

'Father,' interrupted Clarence, 'Jack hasn't done his story on my excavations yet. I was so busy with the shards, we didn't have time to talk today.'

'Didn't want to disturb your important work,' said Jack to Clarence.

'Iris was a big help, weren't you?' Clarence said, beaming at me, then turned to Jack. 'So it's settled then, Mr. Clancy. You'll stay one more night?'

'Well, I'd like to,' said Jack.

'Good,' said Clarence. 'We can get started with the article right after dinner.'

'How about tomorrow morning?' said Jack. 'I like to get started bright and early.'

Mr. Leonard nodded approvingly. 'Real go-getters get going in the morning. Never fails. Start off the day with pep and purpose, and you're sure to accomplish a lot.'

'Has anyone contacted Florence's relatives?' said Jack, changing the subject. 'She must have some relatives.' He looked inquiringly at Madame Sophie.

Mr. Jones spoke up. 'She was an orphan,' he said firmly.

Madame Sophie looked dreamy. 'Well, Raymond, that doesn't mean we can't contact her relatives.'

'But they're dead, if she's an orphan,' said Henry, and then realized what the medium was getting at.

'Well,' said Mr. Jones smoothly, 'if Florence is on the other side, she can speak to them herself.'

Madame Sophie burst into tears. 'Reunited with her dead loved ones. What a comfort it is.'

'Maybe we *should* contact her,' said Mrs. Brockhurst. 'Find out what did happen to her. I can't imagine what she was doing in Clarence's mummy case. I'd like to hear it from her own lips. Well, not her *own* lips actually, but from her.'

'Not now,' said Madame Sophie. 'It is too soon. I'm not at my best.'

'Well, we can wait until you feel stronger,' said Mrs. Brockhurst, although I could see how eager she was.

We took our coffee in the living room. Jack startled me by drawing me back into the hall and announcing precipitously to everyone that he and I were going for a drive.

Clarence stood up, his hands in fists. 'What? A drive? What for?'

'We'll just be gone for a little while,' said Jack. 'Iris wants to take a spin in my new car.'

'Jack *insisted*,' I said unconvincingly as I was pulled from the room.

'Hurry up,' said Jack, when we were out of earshot, 'there's not a moment to lose.'

Right on schedule, Chan, now wearing a dark suit and snap-brim fedora and smoking a cigarette, stepped into a low black car. The car took off, and a little while later Jack, with his lights off, followed. 'There's only one way out of here,' he said, 'so I'll give him a little slack. By the time I catch up there'll be other traffic around.' We waited further up the road while Chan's driver got out and opened the gate, then followed.

It was evident after a while that Chan was going down to San Francisco. We kept behind him a few cars on the El Camino Real, and then almost lost him in San Francisco, but found him again on Grant Avenue.

While we were following the dark car down the principal Chinatown street, lined with pagoda-like bazaars, I said to Jack, 'But we're all the way in the city. We won't get back for hours. What will the Brockhursts think?'

'You mean Clarence?' said Jack, with an irritating smile.

'I'm very fond of Clarence,' I said firmly.

'That may be,' said Jack, 'but this is murder. Or it probably is. A plucky girl like you isn't going to be content sorting shards when there's detecting to be done. If Clarence is the man I think he is, or at least the man he should be, why, he'll know that about you.'

'Well, we could have invited him,' I said, knowing it would have been all wrong somehow.

'Hey! He just pulled into Ross Alley.' Jack brought the car to a stop. In the dim streetlight, half obscured by fog, Chan was stepping out of the car. He put one foot on the running board where he adjusted a spat.

'What do we do now?' I whispered.

'Let's wait a moment,' said Jack, peering intently through the windshield. Just then a door in a grimy brick building off the alley opened, and Chan disappeared into it.

'Man's a regular vanishing act,' said Jack. 'Always popping in and out of doors. I wonder what he's up to. Come on.'

We got out of the car—I didn't wait for Jack to open my door, which was a good thing, as he was halfway down the alley by the time I struggled out. I ran to catch up with him and we looked down the alley.

From the other direction a party of young people entered the alley from Stockton Street. They were loud and laughing and wearing very smart evening clothes.

Jack took my arm and we stepped back into the shadows beneath a fire escape. I bumped against a garbage can and a cat yowled.

'*Sshh,*' said Jack, and we watched the jovial group. One of them knocked on the door and

Jack leaned forward.

'I got the password,' he said to me in a triumphant whisper.

'Is that a speakeasy?' I said.

CHAPTER EIGHT

'I don't get it,' said Jack. 'San Francisco is wide open and wet. There are plenty of places to get a drink. Might be more than drinking going on in there. Ross Alley used to be full of gambling dens, but now it's just a bunch of counting houses for wholesale merchants. As far as I know, anyway.'

'Well, what are we waiting for?' I said.

Jack looked at me with a little frown. 'Maybe I shouldn't take you in there, Iris.'

I stamped my foot. 'Jack Clancy, don't be ridiculous,' I said. 'If you don't take me in there, I'll never speak to you again.'

He sighed. 'Well, come on then.'

We crossed the street and Jack gave a confident rap on the door. A second later a thin slit at eye level shot open and a pair of Oriental eyes looked out at us.

'Happy New Year,' said Jack playfully.

The eyes blinked once, the little opening in the door was slid shut, and then the door was opened.

'Well, that was easy,' said Jack.

101

We went in and found ourselves in a sort of lobby filled with red plush and gold bric-a-brac—Chinese idols and dragons in niches in the wall. At the end of this entrance, through a curtain of crystal beads, a large smoky room awaited. There was lots of loud laughter and some frenetic jazz.

The doorman silently took our coats and ushered us toward the beaded curtain. We went through and were met by a very correctly attired *maître d'* who escorted us to a small table near the dance floor. Jack slipped him a bill, and I sat down to take it all in.

'What a joint,' said Jack. 'Pretty fancy for a little hole in the wall in Chinatown. How come I never heard of this place?'

'Oh, I imagine there are a few low dives you haven't heard of,' I said.

'Listen, Iris, we aren't exactly slumming.' He pulled some bills out of his pocket. 'You have any mad money with you? This might be pretty costly. 'Course the *Globe* will reimburse us. Oh, I guess I have enough.'

'Do you see Chan anywhere?' I asked.

We scanned the room. The place was crowded with gaily dressed revellers, but no one at the tables appeared to be Chinese. The waiters who made their way through the tables were all Chinese, however, as were the two tall men wielding silver cocktail shakers at a long marble bar which ran down one side of the room.

There was a small orchestra, with a lot of horns in it, and a dance floor. Presently the orchestra stopped, and the dancers returned to their tables.

From behind a heavy brocade curtain caught up with thick tasseled velvet ropes, a chorus line of pert Chinese girls came kicking their way out. They all had identical bobs with heavy bangs down to their eyes, and crimson mouths and cheeks. They wore short green silk tunics, embroidered with gold dragons, green silk stockings rolled to just below the knee, and golden high-heeled slippers.

'Boy,' said Jack, 'this isn't any old chop-suey joint. Look at those jazz babies dance.' The girls were now executing various angular dance maneuvers related to the Charleston, all elbows and knees.

'Maybe Chan is working as a waiter here at night,' I said.

'Could be.' Jack's gaze traveled across the room, where he saw a man in evening dress, accompanied by a young woman in incredibly sumptuous furs, disappear behind yet another curtain of crystal beads and climb some stairs. 'Wonder what's going on upstairs,' he said.

Our waiter returned and Jack ordered a bottle of champagne and a dozen oysters. 'May as well enjoy ourselves while we detect,' he said. When the waiter came back he assured us the champagne was fresh off the boat.

'We still haven't spotted Chan,' I said.

'Well, take it easy. We can't exactly run around searching the place. Relax and enjoy the show.' Jack smiled and drank his champagne, but his shrewd green eyes continued to explore the room.

Jack hailed our waiter and asked him what went on upstairs and if we could go there. He placed a few bills on the table.

'Private party,' said the waiter haughtily, eyeing the greenbacks with thinly veiled contempt.

I had given up on Chan; he wasn't anywhere at hand, so I decided to sit back and take in my surroundings. I certainly had never been in such a place before. I found the experience rather piquant. I took a deep sip of champagne and smiled at Jack.

'Now, for heaven's sake, Iris,' he said fussily, 'don't tell your aunt I took you to a place like this.'

'Oh, there's nothing really *wrong* with it, is there?' I said, irritated that Jack should be so protective, and also irritated that he should think I'd never graced a den of glamorous vice before.

'For all we know they've got sing-song girls one floor up,' muttered Jack. 'Champagne does taste like it's fresh off the boat, though.'

Suddenly I thought of Clarence, sitting home with his shards and doubtless wondering what had happened to me.

'I suppose, if Chan isn't here,' I said, 'we should get back. Or at least telephone the Brockhursts.'

'Oh, don't worry about them,' said Jack. The Chinese girls had finished their number and were leaving the dance floor. The orchestra started up again, and Jack took my hand. 'Come on, let's dance.'

I remembered from our time together aboard ship what a good dancer Jack was, so I took another sip of champagne, pushed the Brockhursts to the back of my mind, and we went onto the dance floor. At first I was a little self-conscious in my simple dinner dress, surrounded as I was by women in a variety of stylish gowns revealing lots of shoulder and *décolletage*, but Jack's natural enthusiasm and confidence seemed to be infectious, or perhaps it was the champagne. In any case, I felt quite marvelous and gay.

Jack took me in his arms and we joined the other dancers. 'Iris,' he began, 'there's one thing I've been kind of wondering about.'

'What's that, Jack?'

'Well, you and Clarence. Exactly what . . .'

But Jack never finished his question, because the shrill sound of police whistles cut through the frantic music, the members of the orchestra threw aside their instruments and overturned their chairs, women screamed, and someone shouted, 'Raid!'

'Now's our chance,' said Jack. 'Let's see what's going on upstairs.'

He took me by the elbow and we thrashed our way through a confused group of patrons, stepping over broken glass and spilled drinks.

We took two stairs at a time and saw that the second floor was in a similar state of pandemonium. There was a funny sort of corridor at the top of the stairs, lined with more gilt idols and Oriental bric-a-brac, and off of it, through an open door, was a large room dominated by a large table with a roulette wheel. Amidst the sounds of female shrieking and male bellowing, beautifully dressed people were scooping up chips and scrambling for another door at the far end of the room.

Behind us we heard another police whistle, closer now, and Jack grabbed my hand. 'That must be a way out over there,' he said, 'but it looks like a crush. Maybe we can do better.' He pulled me along behind him back down the corridor, and we careened around a corner. The sounds of commotion in the gambling room indicated that the police had arrived there, and I had the impression we had eluded the law for now at least.

'Let's pop in here,' said Jack urgently, and we dashed through an archway hung with more crystal beads, into a funny little alcove. It was pitch black in there, but we felt our way around and finally found a door. 'Maybe we can hide out in there, or maybe it's a way out,' whispered Jack. He tried the door, but it was locked. Then he stood back, gave the lock a terrific kick and then hurled himself against it. It opened and we tumbled in. Jack hadn't broken the door down, just dislodged a rather flimsy lock. Now he closed the door, and we leaned against it, panting for breath.

My eyes were becoming accustomed to the dark, and I seemed to make out the shapes of modern furnishings—a desk and file cabinet. I didn't see much, though, before the blow to the back of my head turned the office into a shower of stars, a revolving, dizzying display that lasted, as I sank weakly to my knees, until I was plunged into unconsciousness.

*　　　*　　　*

When I came to, I was in an entirely different place. My head ached and I felt weak. I was lying in a damp basement room on a cold cement floor, and I was looking at a labyrinth of steam pipes overhead. I tried to sit up and instinctively wanted to put my hand to my aching head, but I discovered I was bound with heavy ropes. My hands were behind me, and my ankles were tied too. I wriggled around a little, not daring to scream but feeling desperately like doing so, when I heard Jack's voice.

107

'Well,' he said, 'we didn't get picked up in that raid, did we? Got to look on the bright side.'

I pivoted around as best I could and found Jack behind me, propped up against the wall and similarly tied up.

'I didn't try to wake you up. I figured you'd be all right, though. You were breathing regularly.'

'Well, that's a relief,' I said rather harshly. 'Jack, how can you be so nonchalant? We're trapped down in some dungeon, I can't imagine what time it is . . .'

'Still night,' said Jack. 'There's moonlight coming through that window.' He indicated with his head a small, dirty window.

'We have to get out of here,' I said rather desperately. 'Whoever hit us may come back.'

'I'm working on it,' said Jack. 'I've loosened these ropes on my wrists a little. But if you can make it over to me, maybe you can help me.'

We slithered toward each other like snails across that damp cement, and maneuvered ourselves so we were back to back. I could feel the slack around his hands, and I picked at the stubborn knot, trying to free him. It seemed to take forever, but I suppose it was only a matter of minutes before Jack let out a little cry of triumph and pulled himself loose. Then he twirled himself around and untied my hands.

'They didn't do such a terrific job,' he said. 'Must have been in a hurry.' We were both releasing our ankles.

He got to his feet, wincing a little. I followed suit and felt cramps in my limbs from being bound. 'Now, let's see if we can get ourselves out of here.' He explored around the cellar, which was dank and dark, and I said 'How can you be so cheerful while we're shut up in this place?' Then, suddenly, as I remembered, I gasped and added, 'What will the Brockhursts be thinking?' At this, I burst into tears, hating myself for it.

'What's the matter?' said Jack, coming to my side.

'What do you mean, what's the matter?' I said between sobs. 'I've been hit on the head, tied up, locked in and all the while Clarence and his parents think I'm out joy-riding with you.'

'Well, don't *cry*,' said Jack helplessly. He sat next to me, put his arm around me, and then fished in his pocket and produced a handkerchief. I collapsed gratefully into it, and then we both noticed something odd. In the dark cellar the handkerchief glowed, as if it were producing its own light.

'That's the handkerchief I found in the dumbwaiter,' said Jack, looking at it with interest. 'Let me see that.' He took it from me and I sniffed a little and stopped crying as he examined it. 'Phosphorescent paint.

109

Whatever can it mean? Didn't notice that in daylight.'

Just then what appeared to be a coal-cellar door opened, and a man came down into the cellar from the sidewalk. It was a little lighter now, presumably from a streetlamp outside. I stared at him wide-eyed, wondering what our fate was to be. Imagine my surprise when I discovered it was Chan!

'You must get out of here at once,' he said.

'We'd like that,' said Jack. 'Where are we, exactly?'

'In Chinatown,' said Chan. 'A dangerous place if you don't know your way around.' He gave us an ominous look.

'What are *you* doing here?' I asked him.

'I heard about your predicament and decided I must rescue you,' he said. 'I'm sure that's what the Brockhursts would have wanted me to do.'

Jack lifted me up through the coal door, and then he and Chan pulled themselves up and into a narrow street.

'Didn't you get picked up in that raid?' said Jack, brushing himself off. He left unspoken the rather unsavory fact that we had followed Chan.

'No.' Chan shook his head, but he didn't provide more details. He simply said, 'I'll lead you back to your car, and I suggest you go right back to Burlingame.'

'Who hit us on the head?' I said, bolder

now that we were outside that cellar.

Chan shrugged. 'I don't know. I just heard you were in trouble. Please don't ask me any more questions.' He gave us a steely stare, the deferential reserve of the perfect butler gone for an instant. 'I'm sure you don't want anyone to know you were almost picked up in that raid. You ran from the police. I won't mention this to anyone.'

'If we don't blab about your escapades,' added Jack.

'What I do on my night off is no concern of anyone's,' said Chan stiffly.

'But what were you doing *last* night?' said Jack.

'Well, thank you so much for rescuing us,' I said, feeling a little foolish. We had reached Jack's car now, and I saw we had been imprisoned in a cellar several buildings away from the speakeasy.

When we got into the car, Jack felt the back of his head. 'I've got quite a knot back there,' he said. 'Whoever sapped us knew what they were doing.'

'I suppose I had better give Chan a bigger tip than I intended,' I said dubiously. 'Rescuing us does seem above and beyond the call of a butler's duties.'

But Jack was busy examining the handkerchief that had startled us by glowing in the dark. He sniffed it. 'Smells like cold cream,' he said, handing it to me.

'Oh, Jack,' I said, 'we must get back to the Brockhursts.'

It was well past midnight when we did arrive. To my horror, Clarence, Bunny, and their parents were all waiting up for us.

I crept in, looking dusty and bedraggled and wondering what I was going to say. I should have realized that Jack would make any explanations.

He told them the whole story of our travels, including the police raid and Chan's rescue.

'Well, why did you involve *Iris* in your little adventure?' said Clarence sharply. He came to my side and took my hand.

'Because Iris *likes* that kind of thing,' said Jack. 'She's very plucky and a real sport.'

'I can't say I like getting hit on the back of the head,' I protested weakly.

'We were very worried about Miss Cooper,' said Clarence's father.

'I'm so sorry to have worried you,' I said. 'I didn't mean . . .'

'It sounds wonderful,' said Bunny enviously. 'It must have been the Silver Dragon. I've heard about the place. Very demi-monde. I've begged some of the boys to take me there, but no one knows where it is.'

'Bunny, you mustn't ask your escorts to take you to dangerous places and to break the law. There's no need for it,' said her mother sharply. 'You can have a drink right here at home.'

'But you didn't tell me where you were going,' said Clarence to me, obviously hurt.

'That's not her fault,' said Jack. 'I really was going to take her for a little spin, when I took it upon myself to tail that butler. I wondered what he had been up to when he vanished before.'

I decided not to contradict his lie. I was uncomfortable enough as it was.

'Apparently Chan is throwing his wages away on the gaming table,' said Mr. Brockhurst.

'Let's not say anything to Chan about it,' said Mrs. Brockhurst. 'I don't want to upset him.'

'He was awfully nice about rescuing us,' I said.

'I could have rescued us myself,' said Jack. 'I was just about to, when he showed up.

'That Chan is certainly mysterious,' he continued. 'I wish I knew more about him. What was he doing up there?'

We heard a discreet cough behind us. Chan stood there in his dark suit, his hat in his hands.

'I feel I owe you an explanation,' he said calmly.

'Oh, no,' began Mrs. Brockhurst, but her husband silenced her with a look.

'I ran into Miss Cooper and Mr. Clancy in the city. They were in a spot of trouble. I was glad to be able to help. They may have mentioned that they observed me in a,' he cleared his throat, 'rather rowdy establishment.'

'Yes?' said Mr. Brockhurst with interest.

'It is not my habit to patronize such places,' Chan said. 'I'm afraid urgent family business brought me there.'

'Some tong angle, eh?' said Jack.

Chan gave him a contemptuous look and continued his explanation. For Chan, he was being positively garrulous. 'I have a sister,' he said. 'Our family is distressed that she has become a dancer at this place. I went to dissuade her from working there.'

We all stared at Chan with fascination.

He choked a little and then said, 'It is a great dishonor to our family that Ruby should do this.'

'Well, you mustn't worry about a thing,' said Mrs. Brockhurst.

'Yes,' said Bunny. 'Wild daughters crop up in the best of families.' She gave Chan a wide smile.

'We won't speak of this again,' said Mr. Brockhurst. 'Thank you for explaining, and also for your help to our, er, guests.'

Chan bowed and withdrew. I guessed he had overheard us discussing the night's events and decided he was forced to tell his side of the story.

Jack turned to all of us and remarked,

114

'Well, I don't buy that story for a minute—his sister being one of those high kickers at the Silver Dragon. If he's so worried about the family honor, he'd never come and tell us about it like that. I wonder what he's trying to hide? And most of all, I wonder if it has anything to do with the maid in the mummy case.'

CHAPTER NINE

I rose early the next morning. It was rather an effort, as I had spent the better part of the previous two nights awake, but I resolved to behave like a more conventional houseguest for the rest of my stay.

I was glad I went down early, because Clarence was there all by himself, and we could talk. The Brockhursts had breakfast served along British lines, with hot dishes on the sideboard.

'I'm sorry, Clarence,' I said. 'It was wrong of me to go off like that.'

'Well, I guess that Clancy fellow practically kidnapped you,' said Clarence indignantly. 'As soon as we finish my story for his paper, out he goes. I won't let Mother add him to her collection.'

'He didn't exactly kidnap me,' I said, trying to be honest. 'He's just so, well, you know, *persuasive*.'

'Now don't try and cover up for him, Iris. I know you're just being nice. And then, imagine the nerve of him, telling me you *liked* that sort of sordid slumming. Really.'

'Well, Clarence,' I said firmly, 'in a way, Jack is right. I do like adventure. I was actually rather thrilled to be tailing Chan.' I put my chin out defiantly. Clarence looked so crushed that I added gently, 'That's why I'm so glad I met you. I can't think of anything more thrilling than your expedition. We have a lot in common.'

'Yes, I guess we do,' said Clarence, giving me a nice smile. 'But Iris, promise me you won't go off detecting with this fellow again.'

I bit my lip and struggled for an answer. 'Clarence, I don't think I can promise that,' I said.

'Well,' said Clarence huffily, flinging his napkin down on the table. 'I *see*.'

'No, you don't. I don't imagine I'll be doing any more detecting with Jack, but I just can't promise I won't. And I wish you hadn't asked me to promise anything. It seems unfair, Clarence.'

He glowered at me, excused himself, and stalked out of the dining room. I started to follow him, but just then Bunny came into the room.

'Little tiff?' she said, as she browsed among the chafing dishes.

'Sort of,' I said, feeling rather miserable.

'Are you and Clarence secretly engaged?' she demanded, as she sat down at the table. Chan hovered around with the coffee pot, and when he withdrew I replied, 'Well, if we were, and I told you, then it wouldn't be a secret any more, would it?'

'I've been secretly engaged,' said Bunny, happily buttering toast. 'I'm secretly engaged right now. It's the third time. Isn't it thrilling?'

I imagined her fiancé must be Mr. Jones of the lip-rouged collar. Although Bunny's approach to engagements seemed too casual to take seriously.

'Mostly,' she rattled on, 'I keep it a secret from Daddy.'

I finished my coffee in a hurry and excused myself. I didn't want to be on bad terms with Clarence, even though I felt he was being unreasonable, so I meant to seek him out and smooth things over with him. Goodness knows, I had had enough practice in soothing with my father, who was often irritable.

I found Clarence brooding in the library, and I went and sat beside him on the sofa. 'I don't like to see you so unhappy with me, Clarence,' I began.

He put his arm around me. 'I'm sorry I was so disagreeable, Iris,' he said. 'I guess I didn't realize how much I cared for you. We were all ever so worried when you and that Clancy

117

fellow didn't come back. And then Bunny put the most awful thoughts in my head, intimating that you and that Clancy . . . well, I'm afraid I had thoughts that were unworthy of you. Or do I mean unworthy of me?' He looked puzzled. 'Anyway, let's be friends again, shall we?' We leaned toward each other, about to embrace, when Jack came into the room with a cup of coffee.

'Good morning,' he said cheerfully. 'Well, this might be just the morning for me to work on that article about you, Clarence. What do you say?'

'Oh good,' said Clarence. 'I've prepared some notes. Let me get them for you.' He rose to leave, but turned at the door and said, 'By the way, Clancy, Iris has told me she won't be able to do any more detecting with you. I'm sure you'll understand.'

'Clarence! I never said anything like that,' I said.

Jack said, 'Of course she didn't say that. She likes to go on adventures with me.'

He was unbearably smug.

Clarence sighed. 'That's just because she's an adventurous sort of girl. That's why Iris liked me in the first place. I'm an adventurer too. Wait until you hear about my trip up the Nile. Did you know I killed a crocodile?'

'Well, you've got me there,' said Jack. 'But if you're such a thrill-seeker, why don't you just come along with me and Iris next time we go into some opium den or wherever the chase leads us? How about that?' He sipped his coffee calmly.

'Well, I suppose so,' said Clarence.

'Why don't you run along and get those notes,' said Jack. 'We won't go away. I promise.'

Before Clarence had a chance to leave, Bunny came into the room with a copy of the *Globe*. 'In all our excitement we forgot to borrow Cook's newspaper yesterday,' she said. 'Take a look at this.'

There, emblazoned across the front page, was the headline: 'Blonde Found Dead in Mummy Coffin: Was She Cursed to Death?' Underneath, slightly smaller letters proclaimed: 'Tragedy Strikes at Mansion. Beautiful Victim Half Naked.' There was a picture of Clarence's room, including the grinning mummy and showing the yawning mummy case, with a white arrow pointing into it. The caption read: 'Dead pharaoh grins at scene of tragedy.' And there was a photograph of Bunny, demure in a pale gown, with the caption: 'Well-known socialite Miss Benita "Bunny" Brockhurst, one of the first on the scene.'

'There's my old debutante picture,' exclaimed Bunny. 'I hate me in white.'

'This is horrible,' said Clarence, his hands trembling as he scanned the paper.'

There was plenty to be embarrassed by, I

felt, but what had the Brockhursts expected from the *Globe*? That line about 'victim half naked' was really unnecessary, and I wasn't sure the Brockhursts would care to have attention called to their money by the word 'mansion,' which I had always understood referred properly only to a house with a ballroom anyway.

But Clarence was upset by something entirely different. He pointed at the caption beneath the photo of his room. 'Ra-Hotep isn't, or wasn't, that is, a pharaoh. He never was a pharaoh at all. This is all wrong. I'm shocked that your paper would be so careless with the facts.'

'We'll do a retraction immediately,' said Jack quickly. 'As part of our story.'

'I'm going to get my notes right away,' said Clarence. 'I can see you need to be thoroughly educated in the ways of ancient Egypt.'

He attempted to leave again, but this time his progress was impeded by Chan, who appeared with some mail. I noticed he was back in form. This time he had his salver, a rather ornate thing with a raised gadroon border. 'I've placed the mail in its usual spot,' Chan said, 'but I wondered what you'd like me to do with a letter for the, er, late Florence.'

Jack swooped over the salver and snatched it up. 'I'll make sure the police get this,' he said. 'I imagine they'll be searching for her next of kin or something.'

I was dying to see where the letter came from, but I felt a conspiratorial twinge of guilt. Jack, I felt sure, might well act entirely without scruples and read the letter. It did occur to me briefly that reading a dead person's mail wasn't as grievous as reading a live person's, but I wasn't sure on this point.

In any case, Jack soon left, and Bunny and Clarence continued to pore over the *Globe*, Bunny with undisguised glee at the cheap publicity her family had received, Clarence with horror at any carelessness of detail about Ra-Hotep. Finally Clarence went after his notes.

I found Jack just where I thought I would. He was standing at the stove in the kitchen, holding the envelope over a steaming kettle. Fortunately, the help was nowhere about to see such blatant wrongdoing.

'Jack,' I said. 'I knew it. How could you?'

'Don't you want to know where it came from?' he asked.

'Well, yes, I do, but don't you think it's . . .'

'Okay. I won't tell you a thing,' said Jack.

Exasperated and defeated, I snatched at the letter and, I'm ashamed to admit, actually assisted him in peeling open the envelope. The letter, on cheap paper, came from someone in Oakland with the unlikely name

121

of Violet Mudge. There were some misspellings and crossed-out parts, but the gist of the letter was clear. Violet Mudge wrote that she was glad to hear from Florence, that she hoped Florence could get away from the Brockhursts and visit her, and that she hoped also that Florence could see her way to giving her some money. 'It's been hard times,' concluded Violet, 'I know you won't forget an old pal down on her luck. But even if you can't help out, I'd be real happy to see you again, dear. I'm not on the phone. Just drop in. I'm always in, since my leg's been so bad.'

'Let's go over there and pay a call on this Mudge dame,' said Jack eagerly.

'Are you sure we should?' I said.

'Why not? She'll be glad to see us, I bet. The *Globe*'ll make it worth her while.' I hesitated, and Jack looked me squarely in the eye and said, 'Of course, if you think Clarence will dust up about it, well, I guess that's the way it goes. I thought you might like to help me find out what happened to Florence. Knowing something about her might help.'

'I'll get my hat and coat,' I replied, trying to frame some excuse for Clarence, and wondering if I really owed him one.

We took the ferry to Oakland and then a streetcar to the address on the envelope. It was a little frame house with a dusty front yard and some chickens in a coop at the side.

'We're friends of Florence,' said Jack to the old lady who answered the door. Violet Mudge was a thickset little woman with the bad leg all bandaged up and a faded print housedress. She had a shrewd little face painted like a doll's, with cupid's bow lips, beaded lashes, and pencilled brows. Her hair was an impossible shade of henna.

'I read about her in the papers,' said Violet, showing us a copy of the *Globe*. 'Real sad, wasn't it?'

We agreed that it was, and Jack told her that he was with the *Globe*. 'We wish we knew more about poor Florence,' he said. 'And when your letter arrived at the house, well, we thought the least we could do was help you out a little. I'm sure Florence would have wanted that.'

A tear welled up in Violet's eye, and she invited us in.

The tiny parlor was filled with mohair furniture, framed photographs, and cats. Jack sneezed, pushed a large, gingery tom aside, and we sat on the sofa.

Jack's skillful questioning elicited the fact that Violet had met Florence years ago when they had both been carnival performers. 'It's hard to believe now,' said Violet, touching a spit curl at her cheek, 'but I was a hootchie-kootchie dancer. Florence was just a kid, about fourteen or so, when she ran away

123

from the farm and joined us. These mean old farmers had took her out of the orphan asylum and put her to work for them, and they didn't treat her right. She was fighting off the old man all the time, and the old woman used to beat on her.'

So Mr. Jones had been right. Florence *was* an orphan.

'There's plenty like that end up in the show business,' said Violet. 'We become like a family on the road. I took her under my wing. Taught her how to dance. She was a natural. That girl was bendable, I'll tell you. Pretty soon she had her own act, kind of a contortionist she was, all folded up like a pretzel.'

'How did she end up as a lady's maid?' I asked.

'Darned if I know. She wrote me last week, said she was working for these rich folks. Didn't like it, though. After life on the road it must have seemed tame.'

Jack asked if Violet still had the letter.

Violet narrowed her eyes and said, 'I wrote her back real quick hoping she could help me out.'

'My newspaper would be glad to reimburse you for a look at that letter,' said Jack, taking out a billfold. 'Shall we say twenty dollars?'

Violet took the money, gave Jack a wink, and said, ''Preciate it.' She tucked the twenty into her bodice, rose with some difficulty, and went to the mantel. 'Here it is,' she said.

Florence, I saw, had taken the liberty of writing on the Brockhursts' stationery.

Dear Violet,

Well here I am living with the swells. As a lady's maid, and brother do I hate it. It's all supposed to get me some pretty good money, but sometimes I wonder who the suckers really are. And that no-good husband of mine turned out to be a louse, just like all the rest of them. Have I got a surprise for him! Well, if I play my cards right it'll all come out okay for me. I'll try and get over to see you soon. You were always real sweet to me, and I won't ever forget it. I'll fill you in on the whole set up here. Until then it's yes ma'am and no ma'am, sweet as pie, and believe me if I didn't think I could make this set up work, I wouldn't waste my time.

Love, Flossie

'She was a real nice girl,' said Mrs. Mudge. 'She could of gone into vaudeville. Real classy.'

'I'm sure she was,' said Jack. He nudged me. 'Take a look at this. A husband. In my experience on the police beat, you seldom have to look further when someone turns up dead.' He turned to Violet. 'Mrs. Mudge, did you know her husband?'

125

'No, I never did. I kind of lost track of Florence for a while there. She married, I heard that, after a whirlwind courtship, and I heard her husband was a real smooth customer. They had some kind of act together.'

'I wish we could find out who he was,' said Jack. 'Know where they got married?'

Violet shrugged. 'On the road somewhere. I don't know. But maybe I could find out. I got a couple of old carnie friends. I'll ask around. That is, if it means a lot to you.'

'It means plenty,' said Jack. 'Maybe another twenty.' He scribbled something on a piece of paper. 'Here, you can get me at this number. Or at the *Globe*. That's the second one. And reverse the charges.'

Before we left I said, 'You'd best keep that leg up as much as you can. It'll help the swelling.'

CHAPTER TEN

On the ferry back I made Jack promise he would take the letter to the police.

'Oh, sure. No point withholding evidence. I'll tell him what you observed about the girl's feet too. Boy, I'm glad we had a crack at Mrs. Mudge, though. We learned plenty.'

We leaned on the rail, looking out at a choppy

Bay and the grim island of Alcatraz through a light fog.

'Florence didn't wear a ring,' I said, puzzled.

'That's right.'

Jack frowned. 'Maybe she divorced her husband. But that whole business about the carnival got me thinking.'

I wondered if Jack had been thinking along the same lines I had. 'You mean about Madame Sophie and the séances?'

'That's right. Tell me more about it.'

Briefly, I outlined what had happened the first night. When I'd finished I said, 'And we didn't see Little Alice. Not so much as the beckoning hand.'

We both stared at each other. 'Of course,' I said excitedly. 'That phosphorescent paint.'

'That'd make a fine disembodied hand in a dark room,' said Jack. 'I bet Little Alice was Florence. She was small enough. And the beckoning hand was her hand, painted up. What saps we were not to think of that.'

'Someone removed the paint with cold cream. Remember how that handkerchief smelled?' I said.

Jack grabbed my shoulder. 'And stuffed her in the dumbwaiter, dropping the handkerchief in the process.'

'But Florence never appeared as Alice at the séance,' I said. 'Neither did the beckoning hand. She must have died before

127

she had a chance.

'It all seems to fit,' I said. 'Madame Sophie and Jones have been fooling poor Mrs. Brockhurst.'

'After her money, no doubt,' said Jack. 'She practically admits it in that letter to Violet Mudge.'

'I imagine Florence was the one rummaging around in my room, looking for tidbits to put in the mouth of Madame Sophie.'

'As soon as we get back to the house, I want to take a look at the spook chamber,' said Jack.

But when we returned, bristling with the excitement of our discovery, we were waylaid in the hall by Clarence. 'So. Off detecting again,' he said, a scowl darkening his handsome face.

'I thought it would be nice to take a ferry ride, Clarence,' I said firmly. 'I wanted time to *think*.'

This set him back a little, and he abandoned his aggressive posture. 'Oh. I see. You know, Iris, there's something I must tell you.'

Jack, who had been shamelessly hanging around during this solemn little conversation, finally responded to my glare and withdrew.

Clarence and I sat rather morosely on the stairs. I had my chin in my hands. Clarence began: 'I know you're keen to join me on my expeditions. That is, if we, well, you know, if the two of us were ever . . .' Here Clarence took a big gulp of air and pronounced the words, 'man and wife.'

'Oh, Clarence . . .' I said.

'Hear me out,' said Clarence. 'Well, I think you should know I might not be able to go on any more expeditions. That is, our money,' he grimaced with the pain of the well-bred while discussing cash, 'it's really Mother's money, and if Madame Sophie continues to prattle on to Mother about grave robbing, there's a good chance I won't be allowed to go on another expedition.' He looked terribly down about it. 'Iris,' he said softly, 'would that make you feel differently about me?'

'Why, Clarence,' I said with some spirit, 'if your mother won't pay for your expeditions, then you'll just have to find some way to finance an expedition yourself.'

'I hadn't thought of that,' said Clarence. 'What a good idea. Of course,' he added, 'there's still hope. I mean, she hasn't said no, exactly. Just that she'd rather not right now, in light of what Madame Sophie has told her about Ra-Hotep. I wish Father would turn the woman out of the house, but his hands are tied.' He sighed.

'I thought your father came from a prominent railroad family,' I said delicately. By prominent I meant rich.

'Oh, he did. But Grandfather lost it all. He

was wild and spent it all on wine, woman, and song. I sometimes think Bunny takes after him. As a result, his children, Father and Aunt Laura, were left without a nickel.' He sighed. 'Sad, but from my point of view, hardly a tragedy. You see, Father would *never* allow me to go on archaeological expeditions. He wants me to go into business. But with Mother controlling the purse strings, thanks to her family's clever lawyers, I had a chance. Now she's come under the sway of that old fraud.'

This revelation explained a lot about the Brockhurst household. Mr. Brockhurst was unable to exercise much control over domestic arrangements, as his wife had all the money, and control over it as well. No wonder he couldn't get rid of Madame Sophie. And Aunt Laura, now that I knew she was a poor relation, became a little easier to understand too. Her touch of bitterness came from her uneasy status, and her tone of moral rectitude was doubtless a reaction to her father's profligate life.

'But your father seems to be active in business,' I said.

'Oh, Mother finally let him handle some of her finances. He's very keen on this business with Mr. Leonard. If he makes a lot of money in this land deal, Mother says he can keep the profits.' He turned to me, aghast. 'I didn't mean to reveal all these details until things were, er, further along,' he said. 'It's just that I began to wonder if you'd still care for me knowing I may not be able to take you on archaeological expeditions all over the world.'

'Oh, Clarence,' I said gently. 'You mustn't worry about that. We are so young,' I added. 'We have plenty of time to know our minds.'

I almost told Clarence that in any case Jack and I planned to discredit Madame Sophie, but I checked myself. After all, it was hardly proper to accuse a fellow guest of fraud. Still, I felt that investigating the séance room might prove enlightening about Florence's role in the manifestation and be a boon to poor Clarence. Surely Mrs. Brockhurst would turn out the medium when she learned she had been duped.

Our tête-à-tête was interrupted by Mr. Leonard, who came tripping down the stairs. For a man of his girth he was light on his feet, and had the buoyant look of a balloon. 'Madame Sophie is going to have another session,' he told us. 'She says she'll ask that dead maid to tell us what happened to her.'

Clarence shuddered. 'I've had enough spiritualism,' he said.

'Oh, but it's all most interesting, don't you think?' said Mr. Leonard happily. The little man wore an expression of perpetual enthusiasm, and it seemed to irritate Clarence, for he snapped: 'Just wait until she starts telling Mother that Father's projects are ill-advised. Then you'll be in the soup too.'

Mr. Leonard looked alarmed, and I felt sure Clarence was sorry he'd been so frank.

'Perfectly sound, perfectly sound deal,' said Mr. Leonard. 'A great opportunity for your father, young man. Surely the woman wouldn't . . .' But he stopped as Madame Sophie came into the hall, trailing scarves, some heavy Oriental scent, Mr. Jones, and Mrs Brockhurst.

'Oh, there you are, children,' said Mrs. Brockhurst to me and Clarence. 'And you, too, Mr. Leonard. Do join us. Madame Sophie is going to communicate with poor Florence.'

'Another séance?' I said. I was interested in the opportunity to expose the phony medium and her smooth assistant.

'No,' said Mr. Jones gravely, 'I fear that a full-fledged sitting would be too much for Madame Sophie. We are going to communicate by means of the planchette.'

'A Ouija board,' said Mrs. Brockhurst. 'I'm sure it will prove most enlightening. We may be able to hear directly from the poor girl.'

'Well,' said Mr. Leonard, 'the doctor said she had a heart attack.'

'Perhaps,' said Mrs. Brockhurst. 'Perhaps not. If you'd care to join us, come to the séance room.'

We dutifully followed, and when we

arrived we discovered the other members of the household as well as Jack Clancy all sitting around the table. The room was not as dark as it had been before, but the heavy blue draperies were still drawn and there was an eerie stillness to the room, sound being muffled by the thick carpets and the place having a seldom-used feeling about it.

Madame Sophie twisted her knot of white hair into place and refastened a few pins. I wondered how she was managing without her lady's maid.

Mr. Jones explained to us how the Ouija board worked. Its name, he explained, came from the French and German words for yes, and on its surface, in English, were the words 'Yes' and 'No,' all the letters of the alphabet, and numerals from one to nine. Madame Sophie would place the tips of her fingers on the planchette, a flattish wooden affair with an arrow painted on it. The planchette would dart around the board spelling out messages.

'This is too absurd,' said Mr. Brockhurst irritably.

I wondered why he was here. Perhaps he felt he'd best keep an eye on things. Who knows what messages Madame Sophie would produce? Maybe she'd try to squelch his business dealings.

'Don't we all place our hands on the planchette?' said Bunny.

'By only allowing Madame Sophie to touch

it,' said Mr. Jones, 'we avoid the possibility of pushing by any skeptics among us.'

'Keeping the game honest, eh?' said Jack.

'There really is something unwholesome about communicating with dead people,' said Aunt Laura.

'You don't believe this, do you?' asked Henry.

'I don't know what I believe. I just know what I don't like. But never mind me. I'm sure no one cares what I think anyway.'

No one answered her, but I noticed that Grand Duke Boris patted her hand in a kindly way.

'I feel the energy coming through me now,' announced Madame Sophie, and we all fell silent.

We looked down at her rather gnarled hand as it rested lightly on the planchette. It began to move in ever greater circles on the board, until it looked like the woman was stirring something in a cauldron.

'Well, ask some questions,' she said irritably. Perhaps her arm was getting tired.

'Is there someone who wishes to communicate with us?' said Mr. Jones crisply.

The planchette slid quickly over the 'Yes,' and it occurred to me that it was rather like asking someone if they were asleep. If the answer was no, then who had supplied it?

'Who are you?' said Mr. Jones.

The planchette slid around the letters, pausing here and there, and we all called them out: 'F-G-R-D-X-X-G.'

'Perhaps it means "Frederick,"' said Mrs. Brockhurst, happy to believe.

'No, it's all confused,' said the medium, frowning. 'The messages are unclear.'

As if the spirits had heard, the planchette dashed back and forth between 'Yes' and 'No' and finally began again in a more leisurely manner. This time there was no mistaking the name. It spelled out 'Little Alice.'

'And what have you to say to us today?' said Mr. Jones.

'S-O-S-A-D,' we all chanted, as we watched the planchette whirling.

I must give Madame Sophie credit. She didn't seem to be watching the progress of her hand, and wore a dreamy expression, eyes cast upward and rather glazed over. Watching her, I couldn't help but feel that she was a very convincing fraud. She didn't look like a shrewd trickster. She had the wild, strangely lit eyes of the true fanatic.

'What is "So Sad"?' demanded Mr. Jones.

The planchette spelled out 'Florence.' And before there was time for another question the planchette began sliding around the letters, this time spelling out the sentence: 'Led to her death by the curse of the entity who was on this earth many years ago.'

'Picking on Ra-Hotep again,' said

135

Clarence.

'Ask her where she died.' I demanded.

Mr. Jones gave me a pleasant but rather crafty smile and repeated my question.

'In the coffin. The desecrated coffin,' was the reply.

'And how did she die?' said Jack.

'The heart stopped. The strain of it all,' was the reply.

'Seconding the doc's opinion,' said Mr. Leonard heartily. He seemed to find the whole thing a rather jolly parlor game.

'Ask what Florence was doing in my mummy case,' said Clarence querulously.

'Drawn to it by a force she could not deny,' was the answer.

'Now, let me get this,' said Jack. 'The mummy turned her into some kind of zombie and she walked up there, climbed in the mummy case, and had a heart attack?'

'I am only the medium. You must interpret the message yourself,' said Madame Sophie.

'Can't we hear from Florence directly?' ventured Mrs. Brockhurst. 'I don't mean to presume, but . . .'

The planchette skipped around, spelling out the answer. 'Poor Florence is still confused. She has not been taught our ways here. She is sad.'

'Perhaps we should end the session,' said Mr. Jones. He put his hand over his face, as if fatigued. For a second I almost wondered if he were about to weep. There was a little tremble in his well-tailored shoulders, as if he were stifling a sob, and his voice sounded a little husky.

As if on cue the planchette twirled around, spelling out 'Bye Bye.'

'Most enlightening,' said Mrs. Brockhurst. 'Perhaps when Florence is feeling better we can visit with her.'

'Come along, Leonard,' said Mr. Brockhurst, 'let's get to work on that prospectus. We can get in an hour or so before dinner.'

'Time and tide wait for no man,' said Mr. Leonard, wagging a finger and looking winsome.

The others filed into the hall, and I followed, but I felt a tug at my sleeve.

'Let's not leave before we take a good look at that cabinet,' said Jack, lingering by the door.

A moment later we were back inside the séance room. It seemed a little impertinent to be prowling around here. It was close and dark; I really didn't like the room, although I could tell, looking around now, that without all the heavy draperies it would be a pleasant, sunny morning room.

'Plenty of places for Little Alice to lurk,' said Jack, investigating the voluminous blue draperies. 'What's behind here, anyway?' He flipped back some of the heavy stuff, revealing tall windows. 'Anyone could creep in here dressed as Little Alice and emerge into the dark, flit around and leave.'

'I suppose,' I replied absently, pushing my hand between the draperies at the opposite window to feel the amount of space there. Suddenly I screamed. I'd felt something, or more importantly, someone, behind the curtain. I must have leapt back about a foot, and then I got a grip on myself, advanced to the curtain, and pulled it aside.

There stood young Henry, blinking at us from behind his thick glases.

CHAPTER ELEVEN

'Henry!' I said, in the tone I usually used with my younger brothers and sisters. 'You scared me. What are you doing in there?'

Henry stepped out of the space behind the curtains and pushed his spectacles back up the bridge of his nose. 'I guess I'm doing what you're doing,' he said. 'Trying to figure out how those crooks fooled my mother.'

'Well, did you have to hide?' I said.

'Mother told me never to come in here. Interferes with the vibrations.'

'We figure Florence was Little Alice,' said Jack. 'Probably hid behind the curtains here.'

'On the surface that would seem the logical

explanation,' pontificated Henry, 'but I have it on good authority that for the first few sessions Mr. Jones drew back the curtains to show no one was there.'

Jack's eye fell on the cabinet.

'Exactly,' said Henry. 'I've investigated it before, but those designs may have created an optical illusion.'

The boy advanced to the gaudily painted cabinet, ascended its steps, and rapped on the walls, producing a tinny sound. 'This time I've brought something to measure with.'

'Good boy,' said Jack enthusiastically, as Henry flourished a dressmaker's tape. The two of them advanced on the rather ridiculous little cabinet and began to measure.

Kneeling from inside the cabinet, Henry called out numbers to Jack. Finally he emerged, looking puzzled, and came back down the steps.

'There are no spaces in the walls or floor of the thing,' he sighed.

I went over to the cabinet myself and looked inside, then I bent down and looked underneath. The whole thing sat on four curved metal legs. 'What about under here?' I said.

Henry shook his head. 'It's exposed,' he said. 'Someone could crouch there, but they'd be seen, even in dim light.'

I knelt down on the thick carpet and looked beneath it. 'Unless there's a trap door in the floor.'

'Not likely,' said Henry, but he got down on the floor and crawled underneath the cabinet, and I swept my hand over the carpeting. All was perfect except for a small hole near the step. I hoped the Brockhursts didn't have moths. The carpet looked like an exceedingly valuable one.

'What about the step there?' said Jack.

Henry poked around at the base of the step. 'It's all enclosed,' he announced. 'But I don't see how anyone could fit in there.' He crawled backwards out from beneath the cabinet and began to measure the dimensions of the step. 'Thirty-eight inches long and eleven and three quarters high,' he announced.

'Couldn't get a person in there,' said Jack. 'Not even Little Alice. Not unless you folded her up.'

'Too bad,' said Henry. 'I was hoping to find a secret compartment. I need scientific proof.' He was examining the step carefully.

'Hello,' he said. 'What's this? There's a little hole in the step here. Looks like it was drilled into the side. I bet that's where the ectoplasm came out. Perhaps they used some mysterious gas.'

'Well, I don't need scientific proof that Florence was Little Alice,' said Jack. 'Or at least that the séances were faked. What I want to know is what happened to the girl

140

and how she got in that mummy case.'

Henry straïghtened up, puffing a little from the exertions of his inquiries. 'She was killed, I bet,' he said. 'It was the perfect crime, wasn't it? Not a mark on her. Someone around here is the perfect killer.' His face took on a radiant glow. 'If I find out, perhaps I'll just keep it to myself out of respect for the perfect murder method. A mark of real genius.'

Jack and I exchanged uneasy looks. Young Henry was beginning to remind me of Leopold and Loeb.

'You know,' he said happily, 'electrocution could cause a heart attack. I bet that mummy case was wired up to kill her. Clarence won't want me poking around up there, but I'm going to investigate.'

Jack took his arm. 'What a story!' he exclaimed. 'Mummy case wired for death. Murderous currents run through body.'

'What made you think of electrocution, Henry?' I demanded.

He shrugged. 'A switch and length of cord is missing from my electric train set. It's either that or an untraceable poison.'

'I feel sure she didn't die up in that room,' I said. I explained to Henry that the soles of her feet were free of dust. 'And there was something more,' I added, describing the strange wavy pattern I'd seen on the corpse's calf.

'Some kind of a tattoo. Maybe the secret sign of a tong,' said Henry enthusiastically. 'Chan's work, no doubt.'

Just then we heard a delicate cough. Chan had appeared at the door. I felt embarrassed being discovered there, and Henry slumped over, looking ashamed too. 'Telephone for Mr. Clancy,' said Chan, and we all went out. I for one wondered if Chan had overheard Henry's remarks.

In the hall Jack took the phone. 'You do? Gosh, that's swell. Thanks a million. Someone from the *Globe* will be around to pick it up. Yes, there'll be something in it for you.' He clicked the receiver down and bellowed into the mouthpiece. 'Get me the San Francisco *Globe*.'

While he was waiting for the connection, he said eagerly, 'Violet came through with a picture of the husband. I've already got an idea who it might be.' He turned his attention back to the phone. 'Hello, City Desk. Clancy here. Get a man over to Oakland right away. Party over there has a picture I need. Send it by messenger to the Brockhurst place.' He gave Violet's address. 'Give the old girl twenty clams. And run a teaser for the next edition. "Our man on the scene has startling new information about the Peninsula mummy murder. The beautiful blonde victim had a husband. His identity will be revealed shortly. The *Globe* reveals another piece of

142

the puzzle." Yes, I've got plenty.'

He hung up, looking satisfied, and said to me, 'Remember what Violet said about that husband? Smooth-talking type? Had some kind of act? Guess who that might be.'

'Why, Mr. Jones, of course,' I said. 'Why didn't I think of it before?' I remembered his manner during the séance—rather like a stage magician.

'That's my guess, too,' said Jack. 'Iris, I believe we're really hitting on all six.'

Behind us we heard a gasp and a low moan. Bunny, dressed in a smart two-piece golf ensemble, aquamarine wool knit with a band of orange at the neck and in the gores of the skirt, was standing behind us in the hall. 'But Mr. Jones can't have been married to Florence,' she said. 'How could he have been married and engaged to me at the same time?'

Jack and I looked at each other. If Jones had been married to Florence, he had an excellent motive to kill her. He was engaged to an heiress.

Bunny stamped her foot and said, 'Men!'

'Now take it easy,' said Jack. 'We don't know for sure.'

'I'm going to ask him,' said Bunny emphatically. 'And if he was married when we got engaged, our golf date is off!'

'Let me handle this,' said Jack out of the side of his mouth. He took me by the arm and practically shoved me into the library. 'We can't let her tip him off.' He shut the library door on me, and I leaned against it, straining to hear.

'No use getting all cut up if it isn't true,' Jack was saying smoothly. 'How about letting me take you on that golf date. By the time we do eighteen holes, the picture may have arrived, and we'll know. If it isn't true, why then you'll have saved yourself the embarrassment of a jealous scene.'

'I want to know now!' said Bunny.

'Oh, come on, Miss Brockhurst,' said Jack in a husky voice I hadn't heard before. 'This is my big chance to spend a little time with you while you're angry at your fiancé. And, you know, you're beautiful when you're angry.'

'Oh, well, if you put it that way,' simpered Bunny in tones so low I was forced to transfer my ear from the surface of the door to the keyhole. 'I guess Clarence has some clubs you could use.'

'Swell,' said Jack heartily. '"Course I've never really played golf. But you can teach me. It's got to be just like miniature golf, just bigger, right?'

Honestly. Jack was absolutely unscrupulous, making up to Bunny like that. Then it occurred to me that perhaps he enjoyed it. I sighed, waited a suitable interval, and then crept back out of the library. Jack and Bunny were gone, and Mr.

Jones, wearing plus fours and an argyle sweater, stood in the hall looking puzzled.

'Bunny couldn't make it,' I said sweetly. 'She asked me to tell you.'

He frowned and started to say something, but I didn't want to talk to him. Unlike Jack, I've never felt at ease lying. I made my retreat past him and went up to my room, where I sat down with pen and paper and began to write.

Florence, Mr. Jones and Madame Sophie were conspiring to fool Mrs. Brockhurst. Why? For financial gain. Florence referred to a lot of money in her letter to her old friend Violet Mudge. Q: If Florence and Jones were married, with Florence posing as the maid for reasons of the conspiracy, why would she write to Violet that she was upset with her husband? A: Bunny. If Raymond Jones had come to the house with some scheme to gain Mrs. Brockhurst's confidence and then her money, but discovered he could marry Bunny instead, might he not want to abandon his initial scheme and simply marry into the Brockhurst money? Mrs. B. seemed an indulgent keeper of the purse strings. Presumably he could do very well by marrying her daughter. If Florence had tumbled to her husband's involvement with Bunny, would she threaten to expose him?

Or would she simply try to get her husband to buy her off? Was this the money she referred to in her letter to Violet? Would Jones want to kill his wife to marry Bunny? Would Jones and Madame Sophie want to kill Florence if she threatened to expose them?

Here I put down my pen, annoyed with the random nature of my speculations. All I had so far was the possibility that Mr. Jones, alone or in concert with Madame Sophie, had killed his wife. If she was his wife. I really should wait until the photograph arrived. Meanwhile, there was still the problem of the séance. How had Florence appeared? I closed my eyes and thought back to the conversation I'd had with Violet Mudge. Of course. I'd been so stupid. Jack had said Florence could have fit in the step only if she'd been folded up. But Violet Mudge had told us the girl was a contortionist. The step might have been big enough to hold a little person like Florence if she were all twisted up inside.

I folded up my speculations about the case, tore them to pieces, and threw them in the wastebasket. Then I set out for the séance room.

In the hall I found Mrs. Brockhurst wringing her hands. 'Oh, I wish Mr. Clancy were here,' she said. 'There seem to be a lot of men out by the pool. I thought he'd kept those reporters at bay.' She was talking to Chan, who replied, 'No, Madame, those are the electricians. The pool lights aren't functioning. I believe the underground wires may have been torn asunder when the reporters trampled the rose gardens, but it could also be mice chewing the wires.'

I slipped past them and made my way to the séance room. Just to make sure, before I approached the cabinet I checked the spaces behind the dark blue draperies. I wasn't going to be surprised again by someone lurking there. Satisfied that I was alone, I approached the cabinet and knelt by the step.

Suddenly I heard breathing, and gasped. But before I could cry out, hands emerged from the draperies of the cabinet itself and clamped themselves over my mouth. I stared, horrified, and then saw Clarence emerging from within.

'It's me,' he said ungrammatically. 'Don't scream.' He released me, and I gasped, 'Clarence, you pretty nearly scared me to death. What are you doing here?'

'What I should have done a long time ago,' he said. 'I'm trying to find out how those charlatans tricked Mother. Did you know Mother is thinking of giving them some money to start some sort of spirit center? As soon as Aunt Laura told me I hurried right in here to find out what they've been up to.' He rapped on the walls on the cabinet. 'No false walls, though. Sorry I hid, Iris. I didn't want anyone to know I was sleuthing around.'

'It's the step,' I said. 'I'm sure of it.'

We knelt together by the step, I borrowed Clarence's pocket knife, and, sure enough, I managed to release a little spring and the side of the step popped open, revealing a tiny space.

'But no one could fit in there,' he protested.

'A contortionist could,' I said. 'And Florence was a contortionist.'

'That little hole must have been for her to breathe,' said Clarence. 'I must show Mother.'

'Wait,' said a voice behind us.

We turned and saw Henry wielding his tape measure. 'I've just been talking to the electricians,' he said triumphantly. 'And guess what? There's a length of wire missing from the outdoor lighting system. About twelve feet long. If only we could find out where that girl hid.'

I explained that Florence had been a contortionist and showed him the door leading to the step.

'Twelve feet,' said Henry, obviously excited, while Clarence and I watched, puzzled. 'Here, hold the tape right at that step.' Henry made an arc with the tape and crawled around a twelve-foot radius from the step on the carpet, like a human compass. His path led him directly under the table where we had all sat at the séance.

Curious, Clarence and I joined him under the table, on hands and knees. 'There should be a hole somewhere here,' said Henry. 'The killer was a genius, but I am too.'

'A hole? In the carpet?' Clarence seemed completely lost. Henry was ahead of me, too, but slowly the idea formed itself in my mind. 'Electricity?' I said.

'That's right,' said Henry. 'Wire could have been run under the carpet. But you'd need a hole for the switch.

'Oh, here it is, right under the center of the table.' We examined a small hole. 'The switch from my train set could have been placed there and activated with a foot while we all held hands. Then the current would run from the switch, along the wire under the carpet to the cabinet in the hole drilled in the side and through the body.' Henry blinked happily.

'See, the table is close enough to a wall socket. In the other direction you'd have a length of wire between the wall and the switch—to bring in the juice. Probably the missing cord from my train set.

'The next day, the killer would just have to sneak in, remove the two wires and the switch, and there'd be nothing left but the holes in the carpet and the hole in the side of the cabinet.'

Henry looked proud of himself, and

rightfully so.

The events of the séance came back to me. 'That crackle,' I said. 'And then the lights dimming. And going out.'

'Blew a fuse,' said Henry.

'And there was a scream,' I said. 'And then that rapping.'

'Undoubtedly the body in convulsions,' said Henry. 'One of the symptoms of electrocution.'

'What a horrible death,' I said, thinking of the girl trapped in that tiny space.

'Clever, isn't it?' said Henry rather too cheerfully.

We rushed over to the step and peered inside. 'But the floor inside is wooden,' I said.

Henry shrugged. 'Might have used something to line the bottom. I would.'

'That wavy pattern on her calf,' I said. 'I know now where I saw it before. The gadroon border on Chan's silver salver.'

'That would be an excellent conductor,' said Henry. 'And the electricity burned the pattern into her skin.'

'What are you talking about? You mean that girl was killed in . . .' Clarence pointed at the step in confusion. 'Well, that's a relief. I didn't like the idea of her being killed in my mummy case.'

'And Chan's salver was missing for a while,' I said. 'I remember now—I thought it meant Chan was off his form. But it just

150

meant that the salver was temporarily missing.'

'Well, what was the girl doing in my mummy case?' demanded Clarence.

'Someone moved the body,' I said. 'In the dumbwaiter. Jones and Madame Sophie. Remember? They retired early. And Clarence, you and I heard the dumbwaiter creak that night. They hid the body upstairs.' But first they removed the phosphorescent paint from her hand with cold cream. I skipped that detail to avoid a lengthy explanation.

'You mean they killed her?' asked Clarence. 'Raymond Jones and that horrible Madame Sophie person? Good. Let's tell Mother and have her send them packing. She won't want to fund their cranky scheme now.'

'It might be more to the point to call the police,' I said.

'I still think it's the perfect crime,' said Henry. 'Because any one of us could have kicked that switch. We were all sitting here, holding hands, when she died.'

CHAPTER TWELVE

The gravity of what Henry had said sunk in, and we were silent for a while. Two thoughts came to my mind. First, if we were right

151

about the murder method, the killer would have had to know how the séances were faked. Secondly, while Jones and Madame Sophie knew how they faked their séances, they took a risk killing Little Alice in the middle of one of their performances. If things had gone wrong, they would have been exposed as frauds as well as murderers.

'The police must be called,' I said simply. I felt it wasn't right that I, a guest, should do this.

Henry, eyes glittering, volunteered for this task. 'I'll tell them all about it,' he said.

I encouraged him by saying, 'I think it only right, Henry, as you seemed to have discovered how she was killed.' As he prepared to leave I touched his arm. 'Perhaps,' I said solemnly, 'it's best not to discuss this in the house until the police come. After all . . .' I trailed off, as I could hardly bear to voice the idea that someone in the house was a killer.

'Oh, Iris,' said Clarence after Henry had left, 'I wanted this to be such a pleasant visit for you. To think I dragged you into this sordid business. If only Mother wasn't so easily duped, bringing these horrible people into the bosom of the family . . . What must you think of us?'

'Don't distress yourself, Clarence,' I said, and I tried not to wonder what Jack and Bunny were up to on the links. It satisfied me that Jack would be annoyed that he'd been absent while I had helped solve part of the mystery of Florence's death.

And then, for the first time since I had discovered Florence's body, I felt a real uneasiness. Someone in the house, I now believed, was a clever and cruel killer. Our knowledge could be dangerous. I wondered if it had been unwise to let Henry call the police. He was just a boy. But he'd been so eager. I wished Clarence had made the call.

Instead, Clarence and I took a walk in the garden. The poor fellow tried valiantly to take my mind off the case and act as if everything in the Brockhurst household were perfectly normal. I let him talk on, about Egyptology mostly, with me adding just a murmur here and there to keep the conversation going. We proceeded past the rose garden, now being tended by a pair of gardeners. The first seemed to be at work replanting some bushes that had been uprooted by zealous reporters. The second was pruning off bits of broken branches.

We went down the expanse of lawn and on a gravel path that wound around among some large rhododendron bushes. After a turn in the path, I saw a charming marble pergola in the Greek style, partially obscured by the rhododendrons. As we came closer to it, we heard voices. Before we could discreetly signal our presence, a scrap of conversation

153

came to us through the shrubbery.

There was no mistaking the first speaker. With rolls and flourishes, and with his voice agitated and raised, Grand Duke Boris said: 'But we must act now. There is no reason to wait. We might lose it all if we wait.'

It was a second before I recognized the other voice. Without a trace of her habitual whine, Aunt Laura said firmly, 'I say we give it another day or two. I tell you, it's a sure thing. Then we can act.'

What could they have been talking about? Clarence and I shuffled loudly in the gravel and approached the pergola. The two of them turned and looked at us like a couple of startled conspirators, then their faces relaxed into social smiles of greeting. I couldn't help but wonder if the intense little exchange I had overheard had any bearing on the murder case.

The grand duke, clad in white flannels and carrying a tennis racket, said, 'Where is Henry? I was supposed to give him a tennis lesson.'

'Oh, he's up at the house. Calling the . . .' began Clarence. But I trod rather heavily on his foot. We had, after all, agreed to keep our discovery to ourselves until the police arrived.

'Calling on the telephone,' finished Clarence. I smiled, pleased that my hint had penetrated. In some ways, I thought, Clarence would make some girl an awfully

154

suitable husband.

Aunt Laura smoothed out her rather bunchy skirt and said, 'That boy needs exercise and fresh air. Too much brain work is debilitating. He spends hours on those experiments of his.'

'What experiments?' I asked.

'He has some sort of a laboratory up there in his room. Fooling around with scientific things, I'm not sure what.'

At the time I thought that Henry's experiments and scientific turn of mind had proved extraordinarily helpful. He had, after all, pretty much figured out how Florence could have been killed. But later, after the police had arrived and Clarence and I were back at the house, another more sinister thought began to form itself in my mind.

Clarence and I stood in the séance room watching Henry and Lieutenant DaSilva crawling along the floor as Henry was explaining our theory. 'You see, a wire could easily have passed through this little hole here, then under the carpet to another hole, here by the cabinet.'

Lieutenant DaSilva knelt down. 'Hmm. You may have something there, kid. Look, there are little metal filings here by the hole that's been drilled into the cabinet. Looks as if it's been drilled recently.'

'And then,' continued Henry, 'the wire could have been fixed so the electricity

155

coursed through the silver tray and through the body of the victim.' He smiled triumphantly.

'Pretty neat trick if it's true,' said the policeman thoughtfully.

'Ingenious,' said Henry. 'Almost too bad I noticed the switch and cord missing from my electric train. Can't help but respect someone who pulled off the perfect crime.'

'What a horrid thing to say, Henry,' I said, knowing but not carrying that I sounded more than a little schoolmarmish. 'If anybody did that to poor Florence, they are certainly not deserving of anyone's respect.'

Lieutenant DaSilva shook his head dubiously. 'I'll talk to the doctor about this,' he said, and he took a little envelope from his pocket and brushed some of the tiny metal fragments into it. 'I'll have the lab boys check for fingerprints on this box dingus too.'

'I can do that for you right now,' said Henry eagerly. 'I have everything I need up in my lab.'

'Oh, honestly, Henry,' said Clarence, exasperated.

'I think we'd better do it ourselves,' said DaSilva. 'But thanks just the same.'

'There's one more thing,' I said, and I told him about the strange pattern on the victim's flesh. 'I'm sure it's the same as the gadroon border on Chan's silver salver.'

'Silver is an excellent conductor,' said

Henry.

'The butler's tray, eh?' Lieutenant DaSilva's eyes narrowed. 'Better have another chat with that Oriental.' He took a cigar from his pocket, inserted it purposefully in his mouth, and led us out of the room. 'No one's to come in here,' he announced, 'until the lab boys have finished.' He jerked a thumb over his shoulder at Henry. 'Make sure the boy scientist stays out of here. And maybe we'd better keep mum about this little discovery of yours,' he added.

Thrilled, I nodded my assent.

When we left the séance room, we ran into Mrs. Brockhurst. 'Mr. Jones tells me the police have come back,' she said, agitated. 'What is that detective doing in the séance room?'

'Exposing those two frauds,' said Henry, happily.

'What! It's outrageous.'

Clarence took his mother's arm and said soothingly, 'Mother, it looks as if Florence was murdered. The police have discovered more.'

I didn't want Clarence to reveal anything. After all, Lieutenant DaSilva had asked us to be silent about our discovery. I was sure Mrs. Brockhurst would tell Mr. Jones and Madame Sophie, and perhaps everyone in the household. If there were any fingerprints, they could easily be wiped away before the police returned.

I decided I had to do something to prevent that from happening. 'Clarence,' I said, 'why don't you wait outside the séance room until the police return.' I gave him a significant look, and he seemed to catch on.

'All of this must have been a terrible strain on you, Mrs. Brockhurst,' I said firmly. 'Maybe we should ring for some sherry or something. You should sit down and relax.'

'Well, all right,' said Mrs. Brockhurst, consenting to be led away.

'You know, my aunt Hermione is very fond of sherry. It can take the edge off things, don't you think?'

Mrs. Brockhurst patted my hand. 'You are a sweet girl, Iris,' she said. 'I'm afraid with all this fuss going on, we've neglected you. I hope you haven't been bored here with us.'

We sat in the library for some time, nibbling on biscuits and sipping excellent sherry. I was interested to see that Chan served us, so presumably he hadn't been dragged down to the sheriff's office for any third degree on the basis of Florence's gadroon-bordered calf. Mrs. Brockhurst, who seemed to be feeling as if she had been a bad hostess, made a point of being especially kind, and we sat side by side on the sofa with a large family album in our laps while she filled me in on Clarence's past.

'And here he is with Bunny. I guess he was

158

about eight or so.' Clarence stared solemnly into the camera, while Bunny struck a coquettish pose in a little velvet coat with rabbit trim and a matching muff. 'And here he is with the baby.' Henry, squirming in a lacy christening gown, sat in Clarence's lap.

'Oh, and here's Theodosia. She stayed with us for about a year. A wonderful modern dancer.' I looked at the photograph of a sturdily built woman in Grecian draperies and bare feet. She was surrounded by small girls, similarly attired. 'It was most inspiring having her with us. She left to start a harp camp in southern California.' Mrs. Brockhurst clasped her hands together and said, 'People are so *interesting*, don't you think?

'Oh, here's Dr. Van Zandt. I helped him launch his health tonic.' The doctor was a cross-eyed gentleman in a frock coat.

'Who's that?' I asked, indicating a portrait of a rather spirited-looking young girl, peeping out from beneath a large old-fashioned hat. Her charming and lively face looked somehow familiar.

'Oh, that's Laura,' said Mrs. Brockhurst. 'When she was much younger, of course.' The album was an odd mixture of family photographs and portraits of the interesting people Mrs. Brockhurst had collected over the years.

It seemed ages before Jack and Bunny

arrived back at the house. And even then, I hadn't the opportunity to be alone with Jack. I still didn't know if the messenger with the photograph from Violet Mudge had arrived. I wanted desperately to talk to Jack. He hadn't heard anything yet about the sleuthing Clarence and Henry and I had done in the séance room.

At cocktails, out on the terrace off the library, Clarence took me aside and told me that the police had been, inspected the séance room, and gone.

'Well?' I demanded, 'what did they find? Any fingerprints?'

'They didn't say,' said Clarence absently.

I couldn't believe he could be so nonchalant about such a fascinating mystery. At least Henry cared enough to crawl around the floor with his tape measure. Clarence seemed only interested in discrediting Jones and Madame Sophie.

With a sort of sideways nod of his head, Clarence indicated Bunny and Jack, who seemed to be having a giggly tête-à-tête. 'What do you really know about this Jack Clancy fellow, Iris?' he said. 'Bunny seems to have taken a cotton to him. Do you think that's suitable?'

'Well, I'm sure Mr. Clancy can take care of himself,' I said tartly.

'Well, it's Bunny I'm worried about,' said Clarence, unconscious of my irony.

Jack really seemed to be making an awful fool of himself. I couldn't believe he'd be interested in Bunny. I had found her amusing at first, but now she seemed, frankly, a cheap sort of girl. It was rather irritating. Aunt Hermione had often told me what complete idiots otherwise sensible men could make of themselves over very silly women, but she had usually ascribed such behavior to men much older than Jack.

The dinner gong interrupted these rather unpleasant musings of mine. It was after dinner—a rather strained meal during which no one mentioned the police, any discoveries in the séance room, or the death of Florence, which I now felt sure was murder—that Jack made his dramatic gesture.

Producing an envelope from an inside pocket, he announced: 'I have here a photograph of the late Florence's husband. Florence *Jones*, that is.'

Bunny let out a little shriek.

CHAPTER THIRTEEN

I blush to admit that I practically overturned my chair in my haste to get to Jack's side and see the picture for myself. The others at table were similarly hasty, however, and in all the excitement I'm sure no one really noticed me.

Only Mr. Jones stayed at his place, looking drawn, while the rest of us crowded around the photograph. It showed a group of people, members of a travelling carnival. They stood, looking smudgy and small, in two rows against the background of a rather bleak, grassy field with some tents and a ferris wheel in the background.

They were a rather ragged-looking bunch. Florence was visible in the first row, very young and pretty, wearing some sort of Oriental costume. Next to her, in a dark suit, was Mr. Jones. His face had been circled, presumably by Violet Mudge or by whoever had given her the picture. It was unmistakably he, rather glowery and good-looking, and of course younger—the picture had been labelled below in faded ink: 'Some of the gang from Dr. Ledbetter's Show of Shows. On the road in Bakersfield, 1915.' Below that were the names of everyone. Florence Jones and Raymond Jones were clearly labelled. Beneath their names I read: 'The Vanishing Lady.'

The others in the group included 'Ella the Fat Lady,' an ample woman but by no means fat enough to be considered worthy of a slot in a carnival; 'Little Cairo,' a buxom creature swathed in veils and loaded down with slave bracelets; a cheerful-looking girl entwined in a python, called 'Becky'; a swarthy family in tights and spangles, 'The Fabulous

Mancinis,' who were apparently acrobats; a portly old gentleman in a frock coat, 'Doctor Ledbetter,' who no doubt peddled some quack nostrum; and a lean and surly-looking group in work clothes and caps, labelled 'Ed, Otis and Sparky.'

'Not much of a show, is it?' said Jack. 'Ella isn't as fat as my landlady. I suppose old Sparky here was supposed to be the thin man, doubling as a roustabout. Ha ha. I'd have sure locked up everything when this bunch came to town.'

'There,' said Mr. Brockhurst petulantly to his wife. 'You see what kind of riff-raff you've let into the house. It's a wonder Mr. Leonard wants to do business with me at all!' He seemed to regret this outburst and said, as if by way of explanation, 'Really, dear, you do try me so,' then flung down his napkin and left the room.

'Well, Mother,' said Clarence, 'what do you think now? Mr. Jones lied to you about that maid, and so did Madame Sophie. It's my belief they used Florence to trick you, trucking her out as Little Alice.' He glared at the medium.

Mrs. Brockhurst looked confused and upset. 'Poor Madame Sophie, I hope this isn't embarrassing for you.'

'Why should I be embarrassed?' said Madame Sophie. 'Because Raymond was married to that girl? She was a perfectly fine

163

lady's maid.' She adjusted some fringed garment nervously.

Mr. Jones rose slowly, looked glassily around the room and then went to the photograph. Silently, Jack handed it to him.

Mr. Jones passed a hand over his brilliantined hair and seemed to study the photograph for quite a while. Then he looked around the room. 'Poor Florence,' he said simply, and then he, too, left.

Bunny watched him go. 'But we were engaged!' she whined.

'Oh, Bunny,' said Mrs. Brockhurst, about to burst into tears. 'How could you?'

'Well, I didn't know he was married,' she said. 'The louse.'

'I wonder,' said Aunt Laura acidly, 'whether he would have gone through with it—bigamy, I mean. I rather think not. It would have made for financial trouble.'

The Grand Duke Boris practically clicked his heels, drew himself up into a military posture and said: 'Your niece has been dishonored. In my country he would be challenged.'

'To a duel?' said Henry eagerly.

Clarence gave his brother a squelching glance. 'Well, here I think we could settle for just having him thrown out of the house. Along with Madame Fakerino.'

At this Madame Sophie shrieked and looked around, presumably for Mr. Jones's

164

well-tailored shoulder to cry on. But the gloomy widower had gone. Mrs. Brockhurst bustled over to her. 'Oh, my dear,' she said, 'I know how this must upset your vibrations.'

'Or just plain horsewhipped,' said Jack casually, apparently still referring to what fate would be most suitable for Raymond Jones. 'But I think we'd better call the police.'

'Of course,' I said. This time I decided I'd better do it. The Brockhursts were simply not up to the task. I went out into the hall, leaving behind me a jumble of conversation among the Brockhursts, while Mr. Leonard gazed thoughtfully at the old photograph. 'My, my,' he said mildly.

Jack pulled the photograph away from him and, clutching it, went out to the telephone with me. 'Let me just give the *Globe* a jingle first,' he pleaded. 'What a story. Sordid Love Triangle—The Heiress, the Lady's Maid, and the Lounge Lizard. A deadly combination that led to a bizarre murder.'

'We must call the police at once,' I said firmly. 'Haven't you noticed that a murder suspect just walked out of the room? By the time you finish phoning in your story, Mr. Jones could have jumped over the wall and disappeared.'

'That's true,' conceded Jack. 'Of course, now we have a motive for him, and a pretty good one—the Brockhurst fortune. But we still can't prove *how* he killed Florence.'

'We already did,' I said. 'While you and Bunny were out on the links.' I smiled triumphantly and spoke into the telephone. Lieutenant DaSilva was at home, but the police assured me they would call him and he would come around.

As soon as I got off the telephone, Jack seized the instrument and got the *Globe* on the line. 'Listen to this,' he exclaimed triumphantly. 'The mysterious identity of the blonde beauty found dead in the Brockhurst mummy case has been solved. Your reporter learned today that Florence Jones, while posing as a lady's maid, was actually the wife of a guest of the Brockhursts. Raymond Jones, secretary to Madame Sophie—'

His narrative broke off. 'This is a hell of a story to write,' he said. 'It's getting too complicated. And details are coming in all the time. Let me just give you the general picture. It looks like Florence Jones was killed by her husband, a smooth-talking ex-carnival man named Raymond Jones. Jones has been up here posing as the secretary to Madame Sophie, the old table turner I told you about. Well, listen, it looks like Jones got himself engaged to the girl of the house.

'That's right, the debutante. Bunny. A real hot little sheba with plenty of S.A. Trouble was, he was already married, and what stood between him and a rich wife was his poor wife—who also knew about his shenanigans

166

playing the Brockhursts for suckers with the old girl talking to the dead. This Jones must have busted up the act but good.

'Divorce? Well, no, from what I've seen of this Bunny he'd have best struck while the iron was hot. Hell, if I'd wanted to, *I* probably could have got engaged to her on the ninth hole at the Burlingame Country Club this afternoon.'

He laughed in a hearty and self-congratulatory manner. 'I'm just about to find out how the deed was done. We've got a real sharp girl up here, claims she has the whole layout figured.

'What? Yes. Miss Cooper. But soft-pedal her. Too bad a nice girl like that should have her name dragged through the paper with this Brockhurst crowd.'

'Well,' I said icily when he'd replaced the receiver. 'If I marry Clarence then my name and his will be in the paper together. In the engagements section. And not in the horrid old *Globe* either.'

'Yes,' said Jack simply, 'but you're not going to marry that dope Clarence any more than I'm going to marry his dizzy kid sister. Now tell me what you learned about the murder today.'

I took Jack to the séance room and showed him everything we had discovered. The holes in the carpet and in the step of the cabinet. How Florence could have folded herself up in there. How the missing wire was just the right length to reach from the table where we had all sat. How a switch and length of cord from Henry's trainset were missing. How everyone—except perhaps Madame Sophie and Chan—could have depressed a switch beneath the table with a foot, thus killing Florence. How the sounds we heard that night—the scream, the bumping—corresponded to the effects of death by electrocution, how the fuse went out and how the marks on the corpse's calf matched the border on the silver tray that had disappeared at around the time of the murder.

'Oh, Jack,' I said, 'the incense—it was a powerful smell, but maybe it wasn't just the incense, maybe it was that girl . . .'

'Frying,' finished Jack grimly. 'What a story.'

'I was right here when she died. We all were. Oh, Jack, it's horrible.'

Jack took me in his arms.

'Poor kid,' he said, patting me on the back while I buried my face in his shoulder.

Just then the door opened, and Clarence walked in. He glared at us as we extricated ourselves from our embrace and said: 'The police have arrived. They're looking for Mr. Jones. But I see you two are *alone*.'

'Not really,' said Jack easily. 'We've got each other. So Jones pulled a disappearing act, eh? Let's find him.' With a gleam in his eye he rushed out of the room.

I turned to Clarence. 'Have they searched the whole house?'

'I guess so. It seems like there are half a dozen policemen running up and down stairs.'

'Let's search the grounds,' I said, and suited my actions to my words. I certainly didn't want to talk to Clarence about my collapsing on Jack's shoulder—especially not just now when there was a murderer loose.

'I better go with you,' said Clarence, and we set out purposefully through the rose garden and down to the pool. We took the little path through the rhododendrons and made our way to the little Greek pergola where we'd overheard Aunt Laura and Grand Duke Boris earlier.

We found Mr. Jones there, all right. Sitting peacefully on a marble bench. Draped in his hand there was a huge lapis lazuli necklace, part of Clarence's collection. And near his other hand, barely visible in the dusk, lay a heavy revolver. The side of Mr. Jones's head bore a great patch of blood. I rushed to his side, but it was clear from just looking at him that nothing could be done for him. Mr. Jones was definitely dead.

Clarence came toward me, as if to allow me to collapse on *his* shoulder this time, but I said briskly, 'We've got to get the police down here at once.'

'What's he doing with my necklace?' said Clarence. 'And why did he have to kill himself at our house?'

'At least he didn't do it *in* the house,' I said.

'Why, that's my gun,' exclaimed Clarence. 'The one I shot the crocodile with.'

He bent over as if to pick it up, and I pulled his hand away. 'Don't touch that,' I said. 'Look, shall you go up to the house and get the police, or shall I?'

'Let's both go,' he said, taking my arm.

At that moment Jack emerged from behind the rhododendrons. 'My God,' he said, as he viewed the scene.

'Terrible, isn't it?' I said.

'Guess he felt remorse about killing that little wife of his and took the law into his own hands,' said Jack, circling thoughtfully around the body.

'Good riddance,' said Clarence. 'Now if we can just get the old girl sent packing, we'll have cleaned out the whole lot of them and we can get on with our lives.'

'Someone should stay here, just as a matter of form,' I said, 'and someone else should get the police.'

'You're right,' said Jack. 'You two go on back.'

'Come along, Iris,' said Clarence proprietarily, and we went back to announce our discovery.

170

The Brockhursts had been maintaining a strained but civilized state of affairs at their house ever since Florence had been discovered. The latest development, however, proved to be too much for their *sang froid*. While the police swarmed over the pergola and summoned the doctor, Madame Sophie took to her bed, attended by a frazzled Mrs. Brockhurst. I must say, Mrs. Brockhurst seemed to be a pretty good sport about the whole thing, and showed real concern for the old lady, who was now, it seemed, exposed as a fraud.

Bunny had a tearful scene in the library and received little sympathy from her brothers or from her father, who had disappeared into his study with Mr. Leonard and was trying to act as if everything in the household were completely normal. Later, Bunny shut herself up in her room and played the same song over and over again on the phonograph at loud volume. 'How come you do me like you do?' went the song. 'How come you do me like you do, do, do?' It was a bouncy little tune that was apparently of some comfort to her. Grand Duke Boris and Aunt Laura had a game of cribbage. Through it all Chan moved quietly, going about his duties with chilling precision. Jack spent all his time with the police, and I was dying to learn what went on there.

Finally, Jack returned to the house. I heard

him on the telephone in the hall and left Clarence and Henry in the library. They were chortling away at the expense of Madame Sophie and her dead retinue, pleased that their mother was no longer under the influence of the charlatans. I was dubious. We still hadn't heard from Mrs. Brockhurst's own lips that she had lost faith in the medium's powers.

'That's right,' Jack was saying, presumably to the *Globe*. 'It probably *wasn't* suicide. Angle of the bullet indicates someone stood behind him and fired right into his head from a standing position. Tried to make it look like suicide. And there was a piece of that Egyptian stuff in his hands. We can give that some play. "Doom from the Tomb," that kind of thing.'

CHAPTER FOURTEEN

He was silent for a moment, while I pondered this exciting news. Then he spoke again into the phone.

'No, I don't know who killed him. Presumably the same person who killed Florence. But I'm going to find out. Better get Flash back up here. I want to have him get a few pictures of that séance room. Listen, I've got something really hot. I know how the first murder was done. I'm going to write it all up now—it's pretty technical. I'll telephone as soon as it's done. Boy, is this some story!'

He beamed at me happily. 'Is there a typewriter around here somewhere?'

'I suppose so,' I said. 'We'll have to find it ourselves. The household is in rather a state.'

Just then Chan crept by, and Jack flagged him. In answer to Jack's question, Chan replied that there was indeed a machine in Mr. Brockhurst's study.

'Come on,' said Jack, and we went to the study door and knocked. From within we heard the voices of Mr. Brockhurst and Mr. Leonard. 'Come in,' said Mr. Brockhurst irritably.

'May we borrow a typewriter?' said Jack affably.

'Oh, all right,' Mr. Brockhurst replied. 'Then please leave us. We're just about to finish up in here. It's amazing we've been able to get anything done, what with all this fuss.' The two men sat at a large desk covered with papers. A cloud of cigar smoke hung over them.

'How *is* business?' said Jack in a friendly tone.

Mr. Leonard smiled happily. 'Young man,' he said, 'Mr. Brockhurst and I are about to make a great deal of money. Not only that, we'll be able to offer lots of gogetters with an eye to the future the opportunity to make a lot of money as well. When our agreement is signed, we'll be offering a small group of lucky investors a chance to get in on the ground floor in a real-estate development that will change the history of California.'

'I'll call the lawyers first thing in the morning,' said Mr. Brockhurst, 'and we can get this agreement signed. I must say, Leonard, you've been awfully patient, what with all this unpleasantness around here.' He turned to us. 'Did they get the body of that suicide out of here yet?' He shuddered.

'Yes,' said Jack. 'But it wasn't suicide. It was murder.'

The two men looked stunned, and Jack picked up the typewriter and helped himself to some paper, and we left the room.

Jack seemed oblivious to the sensation he had created, and sought a quiet corner to bat out his story. I suggested my room, and we went up there. I strolled around the room thinking while Jack wrote up what Clarence, Henry, and I had discovered about the mechanical means of Florence's murder. I looked over his shoulder as he worked. He seemed to compose as fast as he typed, which he did quickly, although using just two fingers, muttering a few choice phrases to himself as he worked.

'. . . sending a deadly current through the ex-carnival performer . . . the sitters,

174

oblivious to the death agony of the tortured woman . . . ghastly thumping as convulsions racked her frail body . . . ,' and ending with his final sentence: 'What this means is that anyone at that séance could have killed with the mere pressure of a foot, unbeknownst to the others, who witnessed without knowing it, cold-blooded murder.'

When he'd finished he yanked the papers hurriedly out of the machine.

'Well?' I said. 'Who did it? And why? And why was Mr. Jones killed?'

Jack frowned. 'Well, at first it looked pretty good that Mr. Jones killed his wife. Maybe to marry Bunny. But now *he's* dead.'

'Maybe Bunny killed him in a rage,' I said. Then, feeling the need to organize my thoughts, I took a piece of paper and made two column headings: 'Motive' and 'Opportunity.'

'Better make two sheets,' said Jack. 'One for Mrs. Jones and one for her husband.'

I did that and began to fill in the paper. Under 'Opportunity' on Florence's page I could list everyone who had been present at the séance: Mr. and Mrs. Brockhurst, Aunt Laura, the Grand Duke Boris, Bunny, Clarence, Henry, Mr. Leonard, and Mr. Jones. I included myself, but Jack told me not to be silly. Chan had been out of the room, and Madame Sophie was tied up.

I filled in the same list on Mr. Jones's

sheet. 'I imagine some of us had alibis,' I said, 'but everyone seemed to drift off after dinner, and it would take some time to do the checking. For now let's just put everyone on the second list too. Adding Chan and Madame Sophie and eliminating Mr. Jones himself.'

'Okay,' said Jack. 'Although we're interpreting opportunity pretty broadly here. I mean, sure, anyone could have stepped on the switch, but how many people could rig up that contraption?'

We looked at each other. 'Henry would have been able to,' I said.

'He certainly enjoyed discovering the method,' I added. 'And went on about how a true genius had done it. Maybe he did it, then was annoyed no one discovered it, so he discovered it himself.'

'But why would he do it?' demanded Jack

'He may not be entirely normal,' I said. 'Clarence said something about that. And Henry himself said he'd planned some experiments to expose Madame Sophie.'

'Well, there are others in the household who would have liked to expose Madame Sophie and her gang,' said Jack.

'Aunt Laura didn't approve,' I said dubiously. It seemed a bit thin, but I put a notation next to her name.

'Clarence felt the same way,' said Jack. 'The old dame kept telling him to get rid of his precious mummy. Might have been enraged and decided to do something drastic.'

Feeling disloyal, I made an entry next to Clarence's name, and then I said, 'As a matter of fact, Clarence was afraid his mother wouldn't finance any more expeditions if Madame Sophie told her not to.'

'Okay, write that down,' said Jack. 'Still, seems a little extreme. Not that Clarence isn't extreme when it comes to this grave-robbing racket.'

I let that pass and said, 'Mr. Brockhurst seemed upset about Madame Sophie's influence too. He doesn't really have control over the money, except for what he's using in this business with Mr. Leonard. He seemed worried Madame Sophie might try and stop the deal.'

'Well, put that down,' said Jack. 'I still can't see why he'd have to kill Florence. Why not Madame Sophie?'

'Maybe that was the idea all along,' I said. 'Maybe it was wired up wrong or something.'

Jack shrugged.

I looked over my list. 'Well, it seems a little sketchy. The people who could have killed Florence but don't seem to have any motive are Mrs. Brockhurst, the grand duke, Bunny, and Mr. Leonard.' I sighed. We didn't seem to be getting anywhere.

'Unless Bunny wanted to marry Raymond Jones so badly she killed his wife.'

I wrote that in. 'It seems unlikely, though. Bunny gets engaged all the time. And she really seemed not to know Florence was his wife. Besides, I don't think she could have rigged up the whole system.'

'Bunny is smarter than she lets on,' said Jack musingly. 'Maybe crazier, too, though it's hard to believe.'

I frowned at the list. 'What about the grand duke?'

'You know,' said Jack, 'if Florence was snooping around looking for material for the séances, she might have found something out about someone. Maybe that's what she meant when she told Violet Mudge she was coming into some money.'

'Fine,' I said. 'I'll put blackmail next to all the names. Boris, who apparently was some sort of gigolo—maybe that's a deep dark secret—and I think he'd be lost without the Brockhursts. Aunt Laura, although what she could have done to be thrown out of her brother's house, I can't imagine. And Mr. Leonard.

'Of those, the only one with any money to pay a blackmailer is really Mr. Leonard. And Florence's letter to Violet talked about a good chunk of money. Although it might not have been blackmail money . . . What *do* we know about Mr. Leonard?'

'I made some inquiries,' said Jack. 'Fellow at my paper covers all the business activity in the city. Leonard is strictly aboveboard. He's made a pile in all sorts of enterprises. Everything he touches seems to turn to gold. Apparently came out west for his health some years ago and started dabbling in investments. Made a pile of dough.

'Besides,' said Jack, 'the maids say he never left so much as a scrap of paper anywhere. Neat as a pin. So I don't know what Florence could have found.'

'Well,' I remarked, 'you *have* been busy. What have you found out about the others on our list?'

'Nothing that looks like blackmail material.' He shrugged and took the sheet. 'We'll fill in blackmail next to the other subjects, too.' He made changes in a bold scrawl.

'Now let's get on to Mr. Jones,' I said. 'Same list of characters but no motives yet, except Bunny's jealous rage. And I suppose the cast of characters who wanted Madame Sophie's influence diminished could have decided to go after Jones too. But why not Madame Sophie herself? It's too vague.

'If you have blackmail down as a possible motive for the first murder,' I continued, 'we'll have to put it down for the second one too. Florence may have told her husband what she had found out about someone.'

'Good,' said Jack. 'Fill that in.'

'Really,' I said as I worked, 'blackmail

179

seems a strange motive for Henry. If a child has done something scandalous, it can be hushed up somehow and the boy sent away to school or something. And Bunny seems to relish being rather scandalous.

'Mr. Brockhurst seemed awfully anxious to get that deal signed,' I said after a moment's thought. 'Apparently it means a lot to him. It will be his financial independence. He might have been driven to extreme measures if he felt that somehow Madame Sophie could jeopardize it. It seems to me he mentioned that he was worried about her interfering somehow.'

'Maybe he was just worried Madame Sophie would scare off Mr. Leonard. But Mr. Leonard seems an openminded kind of fellow.'

'Mr. Brockhurst might not realize that,' I said. 'He keeps talking about how integrity among business associates is so important. I guess Mrs. B. has really tried him with all her little fads.'

'Let's take a look at those sheets now,' said Jack.

Together we scanned them.

FLORENCE JONES

Opportunity	Motive
Mr. B.	End Mme. Sophie's influence. (business deal) Blackmail?

180

Mrs. B.	Blackmail?
Aunt Laura	Disapproval of the séances? Blackmail?
Grand Duke Boris	Blackmail?
Bunny	Jealous of Florence? Blackmail?
Clarence	End Mme. Sophie's influence. (financing expeditions) Blackmail?
Henry	Madness? Trick to expose seances gone awry? Blackmail?
Mr. Leonard	Blackmail?
Mr. Jones	Eliminate wife to marry Bunny? Prevent exposure? Blackmail?

RAYMOND JONES

Opportunity	*Motive*
Mr. B.	End Mme. Sophie's influence (but why not kill *her*?) Blackmail?
Mrs. B.	Blackmail?
Laura	Blackmail?
Grand Duke Boris	Blackmail?
Bunny	Jealous rage? Blackmail?
Clarence	End Mme. Sophie's influence (but again, why not kill *her*?)
Henry	Madness? To cover first murder?

181

Mr. Leonard	Blackmail?
Chan	Blackmail? (What was Chan up to the night of the murder?)

'Doesn't seem to be much there,' said Jack. 'Blackmail as a motive is written all over, but all we have to go on is that Florence went through people's things and planned to come into some money. Hardly good enough for a court of law.'

I sighed. 'What I find so difficult is that whoever killed Florence would have had to know how the act worked. That would take some time to work out. Yet the whole family hadn't been to a séance until the night Florence died.'

'There's just one thing to do,' said Jack purposefully. 'We must force the killer's hand through some ruse.'

'Oh, Jack,' I said, strangely thrilled. 'What do you have in mind?'

'I'm not sure yet,' he said thoughtfully. 'First, I've got to get on the horn with this copy.'

'Well, after that, let's discuss it,' I said eagerly.

He put his hand on mine and gazed rather soulfully into my eyes. 'Iris, this could be dangerous. I mustn't involve you.'

'Oh *really*, Jack,' I said, drawing my hand

away. Jack didn't seem to notice. He went out, clutching his copy.

I was angry at him for being so condescending and not including me in whatever plan he might develop to smoke out the killer. I was just as smart as Jack at this sort of thing, and he knew it. Without my help he might make a hash of the whole business. I almost wished he would. Irritably, I got ready for bed, deciding that under the circumstances I needn't go down and say good night to everyone. I was simply too tired, and the household was in a confused enough state that I thought the kindest thing I as a guest could do was to go quietly to bed.

CHAPTER FIFTEEN

I slept very late. When I arrived at breakfast I found myself alone with Bunny at the table. She looked tired and puffy, as if she had been crying. I wasn't quite sure what to say under the circumstances.

'I'm sorry,' I said simply. 'I know this has been a shock to you.'

'Oh, Iris,' said Bunny with a little sob. 'What's the matter with me? Why can't I get engaged and have a nice time like other girls? Why does it always end up so messy? I feel such a fool.'

Bad taste in men was, I felt, Bunny's chief problem. Not knowing quite how to point this out tactfully I said, 'Well, you're awfully young, Bunny. You have plenty of time. Meanwhile, why don't you find something to *do* to take your mind off . . .'

'Off the opposite sex, you mean?' said Bunny, sniffing and toying with a plate of scrambled eggs. 'I can't seem to.'

'Well then, maybe you could find more suitable objects for your affections,' I said. 'Take a look at your fiancés. Now that chauffeur, for instance, and Mr. Jones, well . . . I don't know who the other one was, but . . .'

'He doped,' said Bunny. 'Cocaine. At first it seemed exciting. But you're right. I should find someone solid and nice and hearty. Like your friend Mr. Clancy. He's really very attractive.' She brightened up considerably.

'I can't think Mr. Clancy would be your type,' I said coldly.

Clarence came into the room and joined us. 'Good morning, Iris,' he said. 'You slept so late I was worried about you.'

'I was very tired,' I said. 'Things have been rather hectic around here, haven't they?'

'I'll say. That policeman is questioning us all in the library. Father is furious. He wants to go into the city with Mr. Leonard to his lawyer's office. Actually, Lieutenant DaSilva asked me to fetch you girls, and he sent

184

Mother to go get Madame Sophie out of bed. She took her breakfast on a tray.' He smirked. 'I can't tell you how pleased I am the old fraud is being dragged from her bed for a police grilling.'

We went into the library where the household was gathered. Lieutenant DaSilva, who had been rather deferential with the Brockhursts in the past, now seemed to have taken charge.

'Now see here,' he was saying. 'Things are getting out of hand up here. That girl dying of a heart attack, well, that could have happened to anyone, but it looks now like she was killed. And that suicide in the garden was no suicide, as I understand Mr. Clancy told you. We've got two murders up here, and we've got to get to the bottom of this!'

I gazed around the room. Everyone was attentive. Mr. Brockhurst looked drawn and pale, and next to him Mr. Leonard's usual bubbliness was considerably modified. Bunny nervously clutched a cambric handkerchief. Grand Duke Boris and Aunt Laura seemed dressed to go out—he in a natty blue suit with a pale pink camellia in his buttonhole, she in a depressing coat that looked like moleskin, and a gray felt hat. Clarence scowled a little, and Henry gazed at the detective enthusiastically, apparently relishing the experience, his eyes beaming from behind the thick lenses of his spectacles. I wondered where Jack was.

Before the policeman could continue, Mrs. Brockhurst came in, with Madame Sophie, looking rather distraught and disheveled, leaning on her arm.

'Now ring for that butler, please,' said DaSilva. 'I wouldn't be surprised if his Oriental cunning isn't behind some of this.'

Chan was summoned and DaSilva told him to sit down. 'I'd rather not,' said Chan, standing correctly at the side of the room.

'Oh for goodness' sake, sit down,' said Bunny. Chan sat on the edge of the most uncomfortable chair he could find, a high-backed affair of mahogany.

'Okay, now let's go over this séance business,' barked DaSilva. Madame Sophie let out a little cry, and DaSilva pointed a stubby finger at her. 'Yes, you can start. Now what kind of a scheme were you running here, anyway? Where did that girl fit in? And Mr. Jones?'

'It's all right,' said Mrs. Brockhurst gently. 'You must tell him the truth.'

'Ha!' said Clarence. 'I can't believe you really want to hear it, Mother.'

'My gifts are real,' began Madame Sophie. 'I've had second sight since I was a child. They made me do it.'

'Who made you do what?' demanded DaSilva.

'Gifts such as mine can't be turned on and

186

off,' she said snappishly. 'Sometimes I need a little help. Those two, the Joneses, came to me when I was weak. I had been working too hard, taxing my powers. They had a vanishing-lady act. It seemed well suited to my needs. Most of the time I was in an actual trance state, but because there are so many skeptics in this imperfect world, I sometimes felt the need to prove my powers more . . . vividly.' She looked guiltily at Mrs. Brockhurst.

'I know, dear,' said Mrs. Brockhurst softly. 'It's all right.'

'All right?' repeated Clarence. 'Oh, Mother.'

'So this girl was Little Alice and hid in that step of your contraption in there, is that it?' persisted DaSilva.

'That's right.' Madame Sophie looked momentarily defiant. 'It was a deception practiced for a greater good.'

'Yeah, and whose good?' snarled DaSilva. 'I take it, Mrs. Brockhurst, you were going to give these people some money for their work?'

'Yes,' said Mrs. Brockhurst. 'Perhaps I've been too open. But I still feel Madame Sophie is truly a sensitive. She was taken in by those carnival people.'

'Hmm.' DaSilva continued. 'Well, it's your money, but if it were mine I wouldn't give this old dame a dime. That beckoning-hand trick—that was done with phosphorescent paint, wasn't it?'

Mute, Madame Sophie nodded.

Apparently Jack had been talking to DaSilva. It was comforting to know that our theories had been correct.

'Well, Madame Sophie,' continued DaSilva, 'I want to know how that girl's body got into that mummy case.'

Madame Sophie swallowed. 'I can only think the mummy's curse had something to do with that,' she said.

We all were silent and staring at Madame Sophie, who looked rather embarrassed. She must have known that her mummy's curse business was by now wearing thin.

'Poor Raymond was really very disturbed by the whole thing,' she began nervously. 'It's true they hadn't been getting on well lately, but he still had some tender feelings for her, I'm sure of it.'

Bunny let out a loud sob. DaSilva ignored her and continued to press Madame Sophie. 'Just what *was* the problem between them?' he said.

Madame Sophie pursed her lips. 'Florence was increasingly reluctant to help us. She said she had bigger fish to fry. She simply hated posing as a maid. Thought she was too good for it. And she was jealous. Raymond had been making a fool of himself over Bunny. She'd caught them on the landing. In a soul kiss, she said.'

DaSilva eyed Bunny with interest, but his manner seemed to indicate he knew all. It was clear that Jack had told him everything. It was a little irritating to have Lieutenant DaSilva talking so knowledgeably about the case when Jack and I had figured everything out. But I sat silently, glad to hear that all our speculations so far had been correct.

'I understand you were engaged to the fellow,' said DaSilva now to Bunny.

'Yes. I never knew he was married,' she said. 'He was so handsome and charming,' she said, as if by way of explanation.

'And I suppose you were going to join the act?' said DaSilva sarcastically.

'Oh, no,' said Bunny brightly. 'He didn't like working for Madame Sophie at all. I thought maybe Father could take him into business with him. Or he could have just been my husband. There's plenty of money. The only reason he had to take this job with Madame Sophie was because his family had lost a fortune. He was very well educated. A Yale man. At least that's what he told me.'

Bunny, for all her veneer of worldliness, was hopelessly naïve.

'A Yale man!' exclaimed Mr. Leonard. 'How dare he. Why, that's my alma mater. The newspaper man said he was some kind of carnival performer.'

'That's just what he was,' said DaSilva. He

turned to the butler. 'Now what do you know about all this?'

'Nothing,' replied Chan. 'I just work here.'

'Okay. Now about this gun. It belongs to you, I understand,' DaSilva said to Clarence. 'Was it loaded, and where was it kept?'

'Up in my artifacts room,' said Clarence. 'And yes, I guess it was loaded.'

'Pretty stupid, keeping a loaded gun on a peg on the wall,' said DaSilva. 'Anyone could grab it and kill someone. And I guess they did. Unless you did it yourself.'

Clarence paled a little and then he said, 'When do I get my pectoral ornament back? What was Jones doing with it in the first place?'

'The mummy's curse,' said Madame Sophie. 'It's a sign that all this evil has come from having that mummy around.'

Aunt Laura spoke up. 'All this evil, like most evil, has come from plain and simple foolishness. The foolishness of letting these people under your roof.'

'Well, it's not really your roof, is it?' said Mrs. Brockhurst curtly.

Surprisingly, Aunt Laura smiled. 'No. It isn't,' she said. 'It never has been. I've just been another guest. Not as interesting as Boris here, or these fakers. Just a poor relation.'

I had never seen the little woman so forthright. Usually her acid remarks were delivered more unhappily.

'Well, listen,' said DaSilva, 'I'm going to figure this all out. I want you people to know that I think one of you is a murderer, and I intend to find out which one. Any one of you could have done this, so no one leaves until I solve this case.'

'You mean we can't throw out Madame Sophie yet?' said Clarence.

'Well, can I run up to the city with Leonard on urgent business?' demanded Mr. Brockhurst.

DaSilva looked thoughtful. 'All right. But come right back. Both of you. I'll send a policeman with you.'

'May Boris and I have a lift?' said Aunt Laura, pulling on a pair of serviceable gloves.

'What are you two planning?' said DaSilva.

'Just a little private business,' she replied. Boris touched the handkerchief in his pocket self-consciously.

'All right. I'll send two bluecoats. But I want everyone back here tonight. At dinnertime.'

'And when would you like dinner?' said Chan. 'We generally serve at seven-thirty.'

'Okay, okay,' said Da Silva.

'Very good.' He turned to Mr. Brockhurst. 'I'll have the car sent around.'

I was dying to know where Jack had been during the interview—and where he was now.

After DaSilva had left, followed soon after

by the two businessmen and Aunt Laura and Boris, Mrs. Brockhurst said to the rest of us: 'This has all been most unfortunate. But I want you all to know that Madame Sophie is still a guest in this house. I'm sorry she fooled me, but I still believe there is a lot in what she says. And she has given me a great deal of spiritual comfort. Even if she wasn't entirely aboveboard, Madame Sophie was very interesting, and what is more important than that?'

Madame Sophie looked smug.

The Brockhurst children sat around, outwardly chastened. I couldn't help but wonder at Mrs. Brockhurst's extreme concern for their guest, when she had just been so rude to her own sister-in-law. And it occurred to me, too, that if someone had killed off Madame Sophie's entourage with some hope of having her sent away from the house, they had failed. It was clear that Mrs. Brockhurst would tolerate anyone who interested her.

Later that afternoon, Clarence and I sat by the pool in our bathing suits. It was still rather cool to be swimming, but used as I was to the chill waters of Oregon's lakes and rivers, it had seemed pleasant enough to me, once the initial plunge was over. Clarence had humored me and joined me.

'Oh, Iris, I'm afraid things have gone rather badly,' he said.

'Don't worry about it,' I said. 'You

couldn't have known what would happen here this week.'

I was awfully tired of Clarence apologizing for the way the week had turned out. 'I mean, what would we have done if we hadn't had these murders to occupy us?' I added, trying to put the best face on it. Actually I was perfectly fascinated with the case. Clarence need not have apologized.

'When we're back at school next week,' said Clarence, 'things will get back to normal. We can take our walks around campus, and I can teach you how to read hieroglyphs.'

'I suppose so,' I said vaguely. And then, because I was tired of the conversation and because inactivity under the present circumstances was so difficult for me, I decided to plunge back into the pool and swim some more. If only I knew what Jack was up to. I'd seen him just once that day, huddled with Chan in the butler's pantry.

Clarence dove in after me—he really was an excellent swimmer—and we had races and splashed about and had quite a pleasant time. It was rather a relief not to have to talk.

It wasn't until dinner that I saw Jack again. He seemed full of enthusiasm, in distinct contrast to the general strained mood of the gathering. Madame Sophie, apparently now assured of Mrs. Brockhurst's loyalty, looked pink-cheeked and fresh once again, eating heartily and conversing a great deal. Clarence, who sat on one side of her, was barely civil but perfectly correct, and Henry, too, was mindful of his mother's admonition to treat the old lady with courtesy.

Aunt Laura seemed different entirely. She wore a slight smile and spoke little, seeming not to pay too much attention to her surroundings.

'I can't believe Raymond isn't here with us,' began Bunny. 'I believe I've almost forgiven him. After all, he could have arranged for a divorce.'

'Oh, really, Bunny,' began her father with distaste.

As if to smooth over an awkward moment, Mr. Leonard jumped in. 'Well, I think a toast is in order. Mr. Brockhurst and I have completed our business. In the next week or so we'll be announcing a new company, prepared to exploit and develop some of the most exciting real estate in California.' He raised his glass.

'To the success of your new venture.,' said Jack affably.

'It's amazing we were able to complete our work with all this fuss going on. Next time, Leonard, we should hole up at some hotel to do our work,' Mr. Brockhurst said.

'Oh, but discretion was important,' said Mr. Leonard. 'If it had been known that I was buying off huge parcels of land, well, the word would have got out and we wouldn't have been able to make such a success of it.'

'To all new ventures,' said Grand Duke Boris solemnly, raising his glass, draining it and flinging it into the fireplace. The glass sputtered and cracked in the flames, and I thought how strange it was that there should be a fire, even a small one, on such a balmy spring evening.

Mrs. Brockhurst looked shocked at Boris's expansive gesture. The handsome Russian caught her expression, but, to my surprise, simply laughed.

When the dishes had been cleared away and coffee served, Jack rose. 'Well,' he began, 'I suppose this is as good a time as any to tell you the news.' He smiled at all of us, who stared back at him in surprise.

'You see,' he said, 'there's new, important evidence in the case. I'd like to get it all sorted out before Lieutenant DaSilva comes back, and I believe I can.

'To begin,' he began a little pompously, 'let us review the facts of the case.'

'Can't this wait for the police?' demanded Mr. Brockhurst.

'Oh, be quiet, dear,' said his wife. 'This might be *interesting*.'

'I guess every one of you knows by now how the séances were faked. Apparently DaSilva got that out of you this morning.'

'Not faked,' said Madame Sophie boldly. 'Simply dramatized and enhanced.'

'Well,' said Jack, 'some of you may not know how Florence was killed.'

I certainly hadn't spread it around. As far as I knew, only Clarence, Henry, Jack, and I knew about the horrid electrocution that had taken place inside Madame Sophie's cabinet. Jack went on to explain it to all of us. I tried not to be too annoyed by the fact that Jack had learned all of this from *me*. It was just as well he wasn't giving me credit for helping to solve this part of the mystery. It was really rather unseemly for me to have been exploring in that séance room. Instead, I looked around at the others around the table. Everyone was listening raptly, and Jack gave the whole story his dramatic best.

'Well, ladies and gentlemen,' he said, as he finished. 'That's how I believe it was done, and that's how the police believe it was done. And you were all witnesses. A woman's scream, the room plunged into darkness simultaneously as a fuse blew, the thumping of the imprisoned victim, now mercifully unconscious, beating helplessly against the sides of her death chamber.'

'Oh, it's horrible,' said Mrs. Brockhurst, aghast.

'And the police believe this? Seems a little farfetched to me,' said Mr. Brockhurst. 'Why don't we leave it to them.'

'But the significant fact,' continued Jack, 'is that any of you could have done it. Any one of you, except for Madame Sophie here, who was tied up, could have killed that girl with his or her foot while continuing to hold hands with the others.'

'Sounds like a perfect alibi,' said Mr. Leonard. 'Pretty clever.'

'Sheer genius,' said Henry.

'Not as clever as the murderer thinks,' said Jack. He reached into his pocket and withdrew a long envelope. 'You see,' he said, 'I have in this envelope something that will prove whose foot touched that switch.'

I gasped, and then the room was plunged into darkness.

CHAPTER SIXTEEN

I tried to make out what was happening in the dark room. The glow of the fire revealed very little, but people seemed to be moving around the room, and I heard a chair fall. A second later the lights went back on. Jack was holding Madame Sophie by the wrists. She struggled and twisted in his grasp, looking much more powerful and wiry than I had believed she was. This was certainly a different woman from the helpless old lady who leaned on Mr. Jones and, after his death, on the sympathetic Mrs. Brockhurst.

As she struggled she looked over Jack's

shoulder and a smile of satisfaction came over her features. There in the embers of the fire the envelope Jack had waved around burst into flame and was quickly turned to ashes.

From the butler's pantry Lieutenant DaSilva burst into the room. 'Okay, okay,' he said, pushing Jack away. 'What made you go after that envelope? Trying to destroy evidence of your crime?'

'But how can she have killed Florence if she was tied up during the séance?' I said. Really, Jack's ruse was very clumsy. I couldn't imagine what evidence there was in that envelope. If it was conclusive, why did he need to wave it around in front of everyone like that? Perhaps he wanted to create a sensational story for the *Globe*.

'Good question,' said Jack, with a puzzled frown. 'I guess Jones killed Florence, and Madame Sophie knew all about it. An accomplice. After all, maybe Florence was going to expose her.' He seemed to me to be extemporizing wildly.

'I have nothing to hide,' said Madame Sophie desperately. She was rubbing her wrists where Jack had held her.

'Then why did you try to burn that photograph?' asked Mr. Leonard.

'If she could kill someone when she was tied up, she's a real genius,' said Henry. 'A real crime of genius. Make it look like anyone but she could have done it.'

'We should have checked those ropes more carefully,' said Mr. Leonard.

I for one couldn't imagine her crawling out of the cabinet and between our legs to the switch. But we had only thought the switch was there because of the hole in the carpet. It might be worth while to check every inch of that room. Maybe the hole in the carpet under the table had been put there in case we got as close to the truth as we did.

'Yes, I tried to destroy that envelope,' said Madame Sophie heatedly. 'But I never killed anybody. I was just worried that it might look like I had.'

'Because you moved the body?' I said.

'All right. Raymond and I did move the body. I admit that. We were surprised as anyone when we discovered what had happened. The séance hadn't gone according to plan. We had to go look. We weren't even sure she was dead at first. She was still warm. But we knew we had to move her. Away from the cabinet. People might not understand.'

'You mean they might well understand. That you were frauds,' said Jack.

'It seemed the best thing to do at the time,' said Madame Sophie. 'We thought we'd put her in the mummy case for the time being and then later, after everyone was asleep, lay her gently outside in the garden. Under the stars,' she continued dreamily, 'ready to be received into the next life, a higher plane.' Madame

Sophie gave me and Clarence a sharp look. 'We never dreamed Clarence and that girl would be up in that attic room in the middle of the night.'

'So you wiped off the phosphorescent paint from her hand with Mr. Jones's handkerchief, stuffed her into the dumbwaiter, and sent her a few flights up,' said Jack. 'Never expecting two young people in love would stumble onto your hiding place.'

'We thought it was her heart,' said Madame Sophie. 'She'd had rheumatic fever as a child. That's what Raymond said.'

'Well, I think we should take this woman down for questioning,' said Lieutenant DaSilva. 'She hasn't been truthful with us.'

'Well, what *was* in that envelope?' demanded Mr. Brockhurst.

Something about his question got my mind working along new lines. Mr. Leonard had just asked the same thing, but in a different way.

Jack smiled easily. 'A laundry list. Two pairs of socks, eight shirts . . .'

'You mean that Chinaman is involved?' demanded Lieutenant Da Silva.

'No,' said Jack. 'It was just my laundry list. I wanted to bring the killer forward by claiming to have found a vital clue. I figured the real killer would try to destroy it. So I stood up here by the fire. Chan cooperated by providing a small fire this evening. Big enough to burn something, but not big enough to illuminate the room. And he stood ready at the fuse box to kill the lights. I asked Lieutenant DaSilva here to stand by.'

'Yeah. Told me you had a startling development.'

'Well, I think we do,' said Jack. 'Madame Sophie here probably killed Jones and Jones killed his wife. So he could marry Bunny. Then when we discovered Jones was her husband and got closer to the solution of that crime, Madame Sophie killed him. Adding that bit of Egyptian jewelry to make it look like more of the mummy's curse.

'We know they were in collusion. Remember that session with the Ouija board? Designed to make us think the girl died upstairs. Madame Sophie would do anything to protect her reputation. Ironic, because Mrs. Brockhurst continued to believe in her powers even after she was exposed.' He looked thoughtful, and then added: 'Madame Sophie may be mad.'

'Jack, I'm sorry, but your little exercise doesn't prove a thing,' I said. 'Only that Madame Sophie had something to hide and that she was used to moving about in the dark.' I turned to Mr. Leonard. 'What was that remark you just made?' I said softly.

Mr. Leonard's eyes grew round. 'What? About the ropes? I said we should have

201

checked those ropes more carefully.'

'No, before that.' I knitted my brows in concentration. I had to make sure of my theory, the new theory that had just formed itself in my mind. He didn't answer.

'Madame Sophie seems like a good suspect,' I began. 'Because no one else really knew how the séances worked. No one but Madame Sophie and Raymond and Florence herself knew about the hidden step. The séance where Florence died was the only séance the whole family had ever attended. That's been the problem all along. The murderer had to have a chance to learn how the séances worked.

'But someone else could have known of it. Someone from the Joneses' past. They had a vanishing-lady act, didn't they?'

'What are you getting at?' said Jack, his eyes glittering.

'Mr. Leonard just asked Madame Sophie why she had tried to destroy the *photograph*. He assumed the evidence in that envelope was a photograph. It could have been anything. But he said "photograph." Now why?'

'Did I say that?' said Mr. Leonard.

'I think he knew a photograph could provide the vital clue.

'Jack, have you got the photograph Violet Mudge gave us? Of the carnival people? We thought it proved simply that Florence and Raymond Jones were man and wife, but

202

there's more in it than that.' I turned to Mr. Leonard again. 'Isn't that right, Sparky?'

'Sparky?' he said, eyebrows raised.

'A common nickname for anyone who works with electricity. Which happens to be the murder method here. Sparky no doubt arranged for the proper functioning of that ferris wheel in the background of the picture. Of course it was an old picture. Thirteen years old.

'And nothing changes the appearance so much as putting on a great deal of weight. Jack joked that Sparky might have been the thin man.'

'Even if it were true,' said Mr. Leonard, trying to bubble as he had in the past, but failing, 'why should I kill that girl?'

'She was planning to come into a great deal of money. That letter to Violet Mudge is more clear now. She hated the spiritualism racket. Much easier to collect a great sum from you. You see, you've established yourself as a successful businessman. A Yale man with a Phi Beta Kappa key. And Mr. Brockhurst mentioned several times how important the integrity of his business partners was. If he'd found out you were an old carnival hand posing as something else, the deal would have been off.'

'It certainly would have,' said Mr. Brockhurst. 'But I can't believe, young lady, that Mr. Leonard . . .'

'Easy enough to find out,' said DaSilva.

'And we can start with that photograph,' said Jack. He reached into his inside coat pocket.

'Let me see that,' said Mr. Brockhurst. He grabbed the picture and squinted at it. 'Well, there certainly is a resemblance. What do you say, Leonard?'

'I'm a terrific businessman,' said Mr. Leonard. 'I've made a fortune. I've helped others to do so, too. My philosophy of success and right thinking have stood me in good stead. There's nothing wrong with our deal, Brockhurst. It'll make millions.'

'Are you or are you not the man in this picture?' said Jack.

Mr. Leonard put his face in his hands. 'Well, what of it?' he said. 'No one took me seriously until I told them I was from back East and a fancy school.

'I didn't want my whole world to crumble because of that cheap tart. She recognized me. I never thought she would. Then she put the squeeze on me. I knew just how to kill her, and I figured the other two would help me cover it up to prevent their own racket from being exposed.

'I didn't think Jones recognized me or that the girl told him, but I waited for him to make a move. He didn't. Then when you showed him that photograph, I thought he might put two and two together. I was in too

204

deep. If he tumbled to who I was, he would have guessed I killed that wife of his. I just went up to that mummy room, took the revolver, spotted him from the attic window, and went down and shot him. I added that Egyptian gewgaw so Madame Sophie could carry on about the mummy's curse some more. She and Jones were frauds. They should have been tapped for the crime. I'm an honest businessman.'

'Why didn't you kill Mr. Jones sooner?' I said, realizing this sounded a little callous. 'I mean, Florence could have told him she recognized you. Or he could have recognized you himself.'

'She said the hush money I was supposed to pay would make it possible for her to ditch him,' said Mr. Leonard. 'I didn't think she'd tell him. And I left the Ledbetter outfit just a few weeks after he arrived and swept her off her feet. Florence knew me a lot longer.'

'But was it worth it?' I continued. 'You have plenty of money, or so Jack says. What if Mr. Brockhurst did back out of your deal?'

'I would have been so ashamed,' said Mr. Leonard. 'Better and better. More and more. That's the way to live. To stop now, when I was doing so well—it just wouldn't square with everything I believe in. There's always room for improvement.'

'You know, Mr. Leonard,' I said, 'your false character wasn't entirely believable. All this optimism and go-getter business philosophy. That doesn't come from old money and the Ivy League. Those are the sentiments of the modern self-made man. You should have been proud of your abilities. Instead you decided to cater to the snobbery of men with whom you did business.'

'It almost worked. I almost got that old fortune-teller to take the fall for me.' He snarled at me. 'Foiled by a sweet little co-ed.'

Lieutenant DaSilva took Mr. Leonard away. He was sobbing. It was really rather ghastly, but I couldn't feel any sympathy for the man. It was ironic. All along, I'd thought the deal meant much more to Mr. Brockhurst. His own domestic freedom was at stake. But Mr. Leonard, with the crazy desire to make a lot of money and cut a wide swath in business, had been willing to kill.

When he had gone Chan came around with a tray of brandy. We all took one eagerly.

'Well, Miss Cooper,' said Mr. Brockhurst. 'I certainly am indebted to you. To think I was about to stake our whole fortune on the word of such a man.'

'You may have done well by the deal, if you ask me,' I said, emboldened by having just solved two baffling murders. 'Mr. Leonard was a very successful businessman.'

'I can't believe anyone like that could help me make a fortune,' snorted Mr. Brockhurst. 'A murderer. And a liar. Why, he said he went to Yale! Imagine, I almost invested a fortune in some worthless little town in southern California. Palm Springs, it was called. Instead, I'll put it all in the stock market. If Mr. Hoover is nominated and elected next November, I'm sure the stock market will take off, and we'll be in sound shape for generations.'

'Which reminds me,' said Aunt Laura, 'that Boris and I have something to tell you. We thought we'd wait until things calmed down a bit.'

'What's that?' said Mrs. Brockhurst sharply.

The grand duke took over from Aunt Laura. 'Your charming sister-in-law,' he told her, 'has consented to be my bride.' He rushed to Aunt Laura's side and took her hand between his, kissing it passionately.

'But that's preposterous,' said Mrs. Brockhurst. 'What will you live on?'

Aunt Laura coughed deliberately. 'We've done very well in the stock market ourselves,' she said. 'I really believe it is wicked to buy on margin, but so many people do it these days, and we put up what little we had between us—Boris sold a very nice set of cuff links and I had some old bonds from Aunt Nettie—and we've made enough.'

'Enough to live on?' demanded Mrs. Brockhurst.

'Enough to open a Russian tea room and

earn our own way,' said Aunt Laura. 'I'm awfully good at sandwiches. And Boris has experience in this sort of thing. He was a majordomo, you know.'

'Oh, Aunt Laura,' said Bunny, rushing to her side and kissing her, 'you've been secretly engaged all this time. How exciting!'

Laura looked happy and animated, with a hint of the spirit I'd seen in her photograph in the family album.

'Well,' said Mr. Brockhurst, 'this calls for a celebration. Have Chan bring in some champagne.'

'We went up to town today and cashed it all in,' said the grand duke. 'Oh, Laura is such a clever, sensible woman. Just what I've always needed.'

So this was their mysterious errand. And when I'd overheard them in the garden, wondering when to act, they had been referring to the right time to sell their stock! I was happy for both of them and wished their tea room success. They had both spent too much time living off the charity of Mrs. Brockhurst.

Later, Chan came in and handed around champagne. 'We are celebrating the engagement of Aunt Laura and the grand duke,' said Mrs. Brockhurst, now apparently resigned to the idea. 'Please take a glass yourself in the kitchen, won't you?'

'Thank you, madame,' said Chan. 'And I

shall celebrate my own good fortune as well,' he said, injecting an uncharacteristic personal note into his serving. 'I too am about to be married,' he said. 'My bride is arriving any day now. From China.'

'Well, how did you manage that?' said Jack. 'Chinese aren't allowed to bring brides in.'

Chan indicated the fine French champagne he was pouring. 'This can get in. So can Mrs. Chan.'

'Well, you can bring her here to live with us,' said Mrs Brockhurst. 'Can she cook?'

'My wife? Cook?' Chan stood up straight and raised an eyebrow. 'No, madame, I'm afraid I won't be able to stay with you. You see, I took this position in order to learn how rich Americans live, so that my own family—and I trust it will be a large and happy one—will know correct American ways.'

'But Chan, you're the perfect butler,' said Bunny. 'How can you learn anything more from us?'

'To be frank,' said Chan, 'it has occurred to me that perhaps this family has not been the most suitable one in which to learn quiet refinement. But I hope that I have been helpful to you.'

'Well, what are you going to live on?' demanded Mrs. Brockhurst. I sensed a certain reluctance in her to learn that people could survive without her largesse.

'I have been very successful in this country,' said Chan. 'I have many business interests.'

'Why, I bet you own the Silver Dragon,' exclaimed Jack. 'That's what you were doing there!'

'That's correct. And other establishments as well. I'm afraid my duties here kept me away from business, and I had to leave at night upon occasion to tend to business in the city. That's where I was when Florence died.'

'Well, say, why did Miss Cooper and I get conked on the head at your place?' said Jack.

Chan shrugged. 'My employees were overzealous. You had penetrated into the office. I am sorry about the raid. A little misunderstanding with the police. We have renegotiated our agreement now, and all is well again in Chinatown.'

'Our butler—the mysterious owner of the celebrated Silver Dragon. How thrilling,' said Bunny. 'Oh, Chan. You must give me the password!'

Chan turned to Jack. 'Mr. Clancy, if any of my personal life is revealed in the *Globe*, I promise you, you will regret it.'

There was an implied threat there. I supposed Chan was some sort of gangster.

'Don't worry,' said Jack. 'I've got plenty of copy as it is. Your secret is safe with me. Say, you run a swell joint.'

'Thank you,' said Chan, refilling Bunny's champagne glass.

'Why Chan, you're about the most *interesting* person around here, and I never knew it,' said Mrs. Brockhurst.

'Thank you, madame,' said Chan. I imagined he took it as a compliment that as butler his more flamboyant aspects had remained completely hidden.

'Well, you must come and visit us. And Mrs. Chan, too, of course,' she said. 'Edgar, don't you think it's fascinating? Chan running some sort of gambling hell?'

'I should have known he was too good to be true,' muttered Mr. Brockhurst.

After dinner we went into the library for more coffee. Clarence waylaid me in the hall and took me out the hall doors to the terrace. 'Iris,' he said dreamily, 'I'm so glad it's all over—the suspicions, the tensions. They've been horrible. And soon we'll be going back to school. I'll tell you frankly, my family has been too much to bear. I can't wait to get back to campus. Then we can be together away from all this.

'Oh, Iris, say you'll marry me. We can have a nice, normal family—not like mine. And we can live for my work.'

'No, Clarence,' I said. 'I don't think so. I'm much too young. I know you'll understand.'

Poor Clarence. He looked rather cut up

211

about it, so I said, 'you have your work to sustain you. Think of Ra-Hotep.' I didn't want to drag things out, so I left him. As I walked back into the hall, I thought to myself that Clarence hadn't even congratulated me on solving two baffling murders.

Jack was there, leaning against the wall bellowing more copy into the phone. 'Got that?' he was saying. 'Now here's the wrap-up. "Behind the fresh face of a pretty co-ed works the brain of a brilliant detective. Coolly, Iris Cooper unmasked the villain, exposing layers of deceptions, questioning him until he broke down and was led away sobbing." Paragraph. "Miss Cooper looked enchanting in pale green silk, the light catching her adorable chin, slightly retroussé nose, and just the hint of summery, girlish freckles. Her hair, a remarkable red gold . . ."

'What do you mean, I'm overdoing it? Okay, okay. Fix it up. You get the picture. Yeah. And tell Maude on the society beat I've got something for her. I owe her a favor. Tell her Miss Laura Brockhurst, Edgar Brockhurst's sister, has announced her engagement to Grand Duke Boris Something-or-other. Should be good for a line or two. And they can use the publicity for that tea room.' Jack hung up the phone.

'Hello, Iris,' he said. 'Boy, were you swell in there. I could make a habit of solving

212

crimes with you.'

'I'd like that, Jack,' I replied. And then, surprised by my own boldness, I wrapped my arms around him and kissed him.

Photoset, printed and bound in Great Britain by
REDWOOD BURN LIMITED, Trowbridge, Wiltshire